Through Christmas Windows

L. A. Shute

Copyright ©2022 by L. A. Shute, Gastonia, NC

I

"Well, this has been a wonderful evening Shanice," gushed Margaret, "but it's about time to go round up the men and for us to head for home."

"But it's still early. I wish you didn't have to go yet," replied Shanice. "We don't have to go into work tomorrow."

"I know, but…"

"Do you have something planned?"

"Actually, no. I'm pretty much on top of this holiday for a change."

"Then?"

"I just don't want to overstay our welcome."

"You are welcome to stay for as long as you like."

"Shanice, I really have enjoyed this evening and this old-fashioned kind of neighborhood visit. Thank you so much, once again, for having us over. Next time it's at our house. But for now…" protested Margaret.

"You're quite welcome. It's nice to get together without some specific reason—especially this time of year—just to socialize a bit."

"It is," agreed Margaret. "It's a shame folks aren't in the visiting habit anymore. I love these cookies, by the way. I hope you haven't been keeping count of how many I ate." And the conversation kept on going, as it often does in the middle of a long goodbye, but it started to change directions. Shanice used the opportunity to make an additional attempt to convince her guest to stay a little longer.

"Cookies? Oh," noticed Shanice. "The, uh, eggnog didn't last long either," she added. "Looks like there's only about two glasses left. I can't just throw it away. What do you say?" And with that she returned to her plea to stay and visit a little longer.

"You did say there was a little something in it, didn't you?"

"Let's just say it's an old secret family recipe," grinned Shanice. "I hope you're alright with it."

"Oh, I'm fine with it," chuckled Margaret. "Your secret ingredient gives it a little edge and it seems, somehow, to go down smoother."

"So why don't we finish off this pitcher?"

"Oh, alright. You talked me into it. I'd hate to see you have to finish it yourself," laughed Margaret. And she picked up her glass and held it out to be refilled.

"I'm sure the guys aren't ready to call it a night yet, anyway," said Shanice. "I think they're still engrossed in the football game on TV. And those games tend to go on forever."

"It was smart of you to set up that man cave in the den! Now they can stare at that tube for hours and we can still chat in peace! And you know they've been sipping their own version of holiday cheer," joked Margaret.

"Shanice," began Margaret changing the tone of the discussion again, "you do such a great job of decorating and getting into the spirit of the season. I've been wanting all evening to ask you about the miniature village you usually set up. It seems to grow bigger each year. I remember it looking exactly like a little town."

"Why, thank you. Yes, the village is one of my favorite displays this time of year. It kind of gives you a light-hearted feeling of peace, and that everything is right with the world. And you're right, we do add another piece or two each year. It's in the next room. Would you like to take a look at it?"

"I would love to," answered Margaret as the two carried their full glasses through the doorway into the living room.

"It's beautiful," complimented Margaret as they entered the darkened room. She was immediately struck by the soft yellow glow that shone through the illuminated windows in each little building. "Just look at all the different structures. You've got homes, shops and commercial buildings of all kinds. And you've arranged them, again, in the form of their own little town. Do you set up the same pattern each year? I mean does the little village look the same every year?"

"No. It may be close to a previous year's setup, but it turns into its own little village with its own unique design every time the buildings come out of the box. I think that keeps it from getting boring. There's a new little community to explore every year."

"And the whole thing looks so real. The buildings are so true to real life."

"Yes. And they do seem even more real at night with light streaming through their windows. If you study each of them long enough, they seem to become more than just small ceramic structures. They seem to come to life in some strange way or another. I love to just sit, watch them and imagine what is going on inside each building," explained Shanice.

"Going on inside them? What do you mean? Do they open up or something?"

"Oh, no," laughed Shanice, "They're just hollow, inanimate objects. But they look real, like someone lives or works inside them. And sometimes I like to stare at one and imagine who could be in there and what might be going on in their life—uh, if, of course, they were real people, and it was a real building in a real town."

"I think I know what you mean," said Margaret. "You kind of make up little people and little situations to go with the little buildings."

"Exactly," answered Shanice. "Just imaginary stuff that helps bring my little village to life for a few minutes—at least in my mind."

"Interesting," mused Margaret. And after studying the village for a minute or two she asked, "Who do you think lives in that large ornate building over there?"

"You mean the one with the tall white pillars in front and the eloquently draped Christmas garland and wreaths in every window?"

"Yes, that's the one. What's going on inside that beautiful mansion?"

"Well, let's see. What do I imagine is happening in that house on a night like this? Hmm," she paused. Then said, "I believe that home is owned by Humbert Smithwell. He's the very well-to-do president of the bank in town. He and his wife really know how to throw a party! As a matter of fact, he's giving one tonight."

"Of course," grinned Margaret. "A Christmas party would be so appropriate."

"Yes," said Shanice coyly, "But tonight he's got more in mind than just a holiday shindig."

"Oh, what do you mean?"

"Here," offered Shanice as she patted the chair next to her, "sit over here near me and let's peep in some of those windows." Her eyebrows raised, "let's learn a little about the Smithwells and see what they're up to tonight."

II

"The banker had finished dressing for the party ahead of his wife," explained Shanice, "and was already on his way downstairs so he could be in place and ready for things to start happening."

꙰

"I'm nearly ready, dear," Emily answered loudly from her upstairs dressing room.

"Any time would be fine," answered Humbert sarcastically, though a little under his breath. He was not a patient man, though over all the years they had been together Emily had learned how to coexist peaceably with her husband.

Then louder so she could hear Humbert made her aware that, "The guests are starting to arrive."

"Yes, dear. I won't be long," his wife assured him "He's such a stickler for schedules and details," she thought to herself. She knew that there was no distracting him once he's got something big into his craw. He was going to spend the whole night checking and double checking everything. But Emily had no doubts that everything this evening was going to be just fine.

"Come in Roland," she heard her husband's loud voice boom up from the front door downstairs.

"Glad to see you, old man," chuckled Humbert. "Thank you for coming tonight, Madeline, you look wonderful. Here, let Jarvis help you with your wraps."

"This is one party we wouldn't have missed," beamed Roland. "Thanks for including us."

"Absolutely. Emily will be down in a minute but please make yourselves at home in the meantime. The bar tender will fix you up with some holiday refreshment in the next room. Just name your drink. Oh, excuse me, I have to watch the door until Jarvis gets back."

"Emily," exclaimed Madeline excitedly as she noticed her hostess descending the stairway.

"So good to see you again, Madeline," returned Emily. "You look very nice tonight."

"Thank you, but you. Look at you! You look stunning in that gown. And I must say, that tuxedo does wonders for Humbert, uh, or do I mean he does wonders for that tuxedo?" She covered her mouth and nose with her gloved hand and snickered at her little joke. "At any rate he is gorgeous! You lucky girl, you," she winked. Emily just smiled a little as Madeline moved on past.

"Oh, Emily," called Bea as she rushed over. "Emily your home is absolutely gorgeous. You've outdone yourself this year."

"Thank you, Bea. I've had a lot of good help. Have you seen the trees?"

"Trees? Just one. Are there more?"

"Fourteen in all. One in every room of the house. Oh, not the bathrooms, of course. That would be kind of ostentatious, don't you think?" Emily's response was made in all seriousness. She could have chuckled and played it as a little tongue-in-cheek, but that never occurred to her. In her mind she was just making conversation. Bea, and everyone else who had overheard her, smiled broadly but quietly giggled politely knowing Emily's sense of humor or rather lack of one. "Please feel free to explore the whole house and enjoy the decorations," Emily continued.

"Fourteen! My goodness! And look at that long, long table set for dinner. So festive and inviting," Bea went on. "How many guests are you expecting?"

"Oh, you mean because there are so many places set? Well, you're right," smiled Emily gratuitously, "not everyone will be able to fit around that table. We've had to set a second one in the next room," she said matter-of-factly but, again, with a smile, "but when it's time we'll open up the retractable wall, so we'll all, essentially, be together." Emily raised her hand and gently touched Bea's arm. "Dinner will be served at 11:00," she continued. "We're featuring a Pheasant *Souvarov*. But please enjoy plenty of hors d'oeuvres until then. The caviars are on the table along the far wall. Celia is helping us tonight. She will be happy to serve you."

Emily then moved graciously on, to mingle with her guests making sure to speak to each one individually so that she didn't slight a single one of them. She always played the consummate hostess at affairs like this, and she had the role down pat.

"I think everyone is having a wonderful time," Jackson confided loudly to Humbert as the hour drew on, the party grew merrier and holiday spirits of all kinds began to soar. "It's a great holiday. Everyone's favorite, I think."

Humbert smiled broadly, patted Jackson on the shoulder and moved away.

The crowd in the room grew as the evening moved along. It consisted of Humbert's handpicked cronies from Chesterton, twenty miles away, and the small towns and villages that surrounded it. Consumption of various refreshments increased. Guests circulated through the rooms, formed themselves into pairs or small groups that were soon disbanded and then reformed into new pairs. Everyone knew everyone else, and everyone knew the reason for this party. Anticipation was high and excitement prevailed.

"Emily," was the summons heard from an approaching guest, but further salutations were disrupted by the booming voice of her husband receiving the late arrival of another guest.

"Ladies and Gentlemen, please welcome our special guest for the evening, Mr. Wilson Squire," Humbert announced. Then playing to his own ego Humbert continued to speak to his new guest in a loud voice so the whole room could hear. "Wilson," he said as he ushered the newcomer into the bustling room, "please feel comfortable in our home. There are a lot of people here anxious to get to know you better so please circulate as you feel appropriate." Humbert stepped back with a slight bow to give his new guest full access to the assemblage.

"It's starting to get late," whispered Emily to her husband a short time later as she sided up to him in a semi-private corner of the crowded room. "I think we need to get on with things before we serve dinner."

"Right you are, Honey," agreed Humbert. "I think everyone is sufficiently, uh, prepared by now to be very responsive. It's time for a speech."

"Ladies and Gentlemen. Ladies and Gentlemen," repeated Humbert a few times until he got the quiet attention of the room. "I would like to ask a very busy man to say a few words to the whole group of us and maybe answer a few more questions. So, with his permission, I turn the floor over to Mr. Wilson Squire, our next elective representative to the statehouse."

"Nicely orchestrated," whispered Emily quite seriously to her husband. Continuing in her assumed role of supporting wife she added, "who knows, dear, this may be your entry into politics."

"... and so, I ask for your vote and your help. Together we can add a local voice to the state capital in the next election," Wilson concluded after a brief speech. He followed with a huge smile and hands above his head raised in response to a raucous round of whistles and applause.

"We got 'em!" said Humbert quietly to himself and he offered Emily his arm just as a gong sounded announcing dinner. The two of them led their guests into the dining rooms.

"Look," he noticed and nodded to his wife, "they are all trying to maintain some measure of decorum, but they seem to be having some difficulty." He chuckled as if that all suited his purpose. "I think, with a good meal and a little more wine, we will be sufficiently ready to wrap up this fund-raising event on a high and successful note."

"Yes," agreed Emily, "I suspect we shall raise a good deal more than just the $500 per plate we charged to attend. People seem amenable to donating money to charities, particularly at this year-end time of year. So why shouldn't they consider ours a charity and donate to it?"

"Us a charity? Hmm," wondered Humbert to himself with a wry half-smile. "I wonder. Could we be?"

But then his mind began to wander and as he contemplated his empty wine glass, visions of political sugarplums began to dance in Humbert's head.

❧

"Oh!" gasped Margaret a little surprised at the story's ending. Then she chuckled. "I see a little better now what you mean about what could be going on behind those glowing windows." After a short pause she asked, "Can I try one?"

"Of course you can," authorized Shanice. "Try that small craft store over there. See what you can do with it. What do you think might be happening inside?"

"Hmm," Margaret gave it some thought for a few minutes. "I think I may know," she answered finally, "But I'm only going to look through those lighted windows on the top floor."

"The top floor? Why?"

"Because they strike me as being the windows of a small, rented apartment up over the shop."

"Ahh," mused Shanice as she sipped her drink. "Interesting idea."

III

"Here, take a look with me," invited Margaret. "Quiet now, so we can hear what the girl is saying."

❦

"Wow! Here we are, Martin," gushed Robin, "our first Christmas together. Isn't it great? I just can't get over it."

"Yeah, here we are," acknowledged Martin in a tone much less enthusiastic than that of his recently new wife.

"Martin!" scolded Robin. "Come on! Be happy. We're alone and starting life on our own and it's Christmas. It's just us against the world and I'm excited."

"I'm sorry, Robin," he apologized pulling her into his arms to give her a long and comfortable hug, "I'm excited, too. Really! You're right it's our first Christmas together and that makes it very special."

"I think we were very lucky to have found this furnished apartment at this time of year. And it's pretty reasonably priced," said Robin looking up at him.

"Well," considered Martin, "Furnished? Yes, but sparsely. Reasonably priced? Yes, but it took practically every penny we had to put down the deposit. Lucky to find it? Yes. Yes, we were! And, all that considered, it fits us just right for the moment!" and he smiled and squeezed her just a little tighter.

"It's not luxurious," agreed Robin, "but it's got everything we need," and she pushed back away from her young husband.

"What we need," laughed Martin, "is some money. Honey, we're flat broke."

"I know," said Robin. "It'll probably be a hard couple of weeks but as soon as school starts back after the holiday break, I'll start my new teaching job and that should bring in some money."

"I wish I could be adding something to the cash box," complained Martin, "but no one is hiring any more until after the first of the year. You're just going to have to support me for a while," he grinned.

"Martin," she said a little crossly, "let's not go through that again. We agreed that each of us would follow whoever got the first job. That happened to be me." Then, in a little softer and more encouraging tone she continued, "You'll find a good job very soon. It won't take long when employers realize what a good man you are."

"Yeah, I know. So far, though, it seems like there's just no demand out there for an entry-level accountant."

"You just haven't hit on it yet. Like you said, things should get better after the holidays are over and places get back to work."

"Yeah," replied Martin without much certainty. "I'll start my internet search again from this new location. By the way, where are we? We drove for days to get here. Left all our friends and families so far behind we'll never get together very much—like at Christmas. This is certainly no metropolis. You've just today seen the school for the first time, where you're going to work, and you haven't even been inside it yet. You haven't met any of the other teachers or staff or your principal. You were interviewed and hired over the internet. We have no idea what we've gotten into or what's ahead of us. What have we done, Robin?"

"We've taken our first baby steps together, Martin. The mystery of uncertainty is what makes this whole adventure exciting. At first glance, this is a very nice, quaint little town. It's small but not too small, and it's within commuting distance of a big, major city, where I'm sure they employ many accountants, even entry-level ones. Let's see where life takes us from here."

"I'd feel better if I had a job, or at least the strong possibility of one. I'm just ready to get on with it but I have to sit and wait out this holiday before I can do anything about it. I'm just anxious, I guess."

"I know," smiled Robin, "Look. It's Christmas and we're in our first new home. Let's make the best of it. I'll bet this is one Christmas we will always remember."

"Hmm," thought Martin out loud and he turned on a slightly sarcastic but humorous tone of voice. "No friends, no tree, no decorations, no gifts, no big dinner, no money. I have no doubt this is one Christmas we will always remember." And he laughed to show Robin that he was teasing her a little bit. He didn't need an argument or a scolding right now.

"Forget everything we don't have. Think about what we do have."

"Right! Uh, like what?"

"Martin!" she rebuffed him mildly. "We have each other. We have a warm place to stay. We have a whole new beautiful little village to explore with all of its lights and decorations. We can enjoy them. We agreed that there would be no gift exchange this year." And she abruptly paused and lightened her mood even more to joke, "No gift exchange so we could save enough money for a nice take-out Chinese Christmas dinner." And she laughed thinking about the whole idea. Martin was taken a bit by surprise and ended up joining in the laughter.

"Right," he said. Then after pacing aimlessly for a few minutes through their few small rooms he announced, "Listen, I'm going out for a little walk."

"OK. You probably need some time alone to sort everything out in your head."

"Yeah," and Martin pulled on his heavy coat and left the apartment.

Robin used the quiet time to straighten out a few things and put away a few others that had not been unpacked yet. Then, because there was no recliner or overstuffed easy chair in the place, she settled back on the bed where she could put her feet up and just relax for a while.

"Robin, I'm back," Martin called less than an hour later as he opened the door to the little apartment. "Come here and look at this."

"What is it?" asked Robin as she stepped out of the bedroom carrying her cell phone.

"While I was walking, I found this armload of greens that someone had apparently trimmed off a tree or a wreath or something. They were just tossed out in the woods. They seem to be fresh, and I thought they might give the place a little of the, oh, you know, a little of the uh, aroma of Christmas at least."

"Great idea. Here, let's use them as a centerpiece on the table," and she took them and arranged them as dramatically as possible in the center of their one table. "There it looks cheerier already. But what is that you've got in the bag? Remember we agreed no presents this year. You didn't spend money on something we don't need, did you?"

"No."

"Well, then?"

"Well, on my way back home, Mrs. Mapleton motioned me into the shop as I passed the front window."

"Mrs. Mapleton?"

"Yeah, Our Landlady."

"Oh, right. I forgot her name for a minute."

"Well, anyway, she gave me this. Called it a little house-warming gift. She said she remembered how much you had liked it and kept coming back to look at it in the shop when we came by to see about renting the apartment. She explained the large majority of her December business occurs early in the month and tapers off drastically until after the first of the year. She said it has become her custom to close up shop a few days before Christmas and go quietly away somewhere by herself for a break. She's getting ready to close the store and, apparently, this hadn't sold. She wanted us to have it."

"What is it?"

"Here, you open it."

"Oh, Martin, I can't believe it," cried Robin as she peered into the bag and her eyes moistened. "It's that beautiful little decorative bell. Here, let's nestle it in the greens." Then there was a long spell of silence as she stepped back and admired her handiwork.

"Martin," she finally said, "we need to keep this forever and place it on our Christmas tree every year from now on. This is us."

"OK. Yeah. Great idea," Martin shrugged somewhat emotionally.

"Oh, I almost forgot," Robin continued. "While you were out, I got a phone call from the assistant principal at the school where I'll be working. She wanted to see if we had gotten to town yet. We got invited to come to a holiday reception that she's hosting for all the school staff."

"Hmm, that sounds like a good way to pass some time. Will there be food?"

"I don't know. But its this evening."

"Then I vote we go," laughed Martin.

A few hours later the two were welcomed into the school's gymnasium where the reception was being held. They did not have to wait to be noticed.

"It's Robin?" asked one of the women later at the reception as she walked over to say hello.

"Yes."

"What a pretty name. I'm so glad to meet you. I think you'll like it here in town and at the school."

"Why, thank you, Mrs. uh,"

"Oh, I'm sorry. It's Edna. Edna Goforth. Please call me Edna."

"Well, thank you, uh, Edna," and Robin smiled a little.

"Isn't this a nice reception that Mrs. Ivy put together?"

"Yes, it is. I'm glad she included us and I'm grateful to be able to meet a few of the teachers and staff."

"May I ask where you are staying?"

"We were lucky enough to rent the rooms above Mrs. Mapleton's store downtown."

"Oh, I see," replied Edna seemingly taken aback a little bit by Robin's answer.

Robin caught the surprise in her tone and hastily continued, "Right now it's about all we can afford. But it's quite satisfactory. Actually, it's very cozy."

Edna quickly realized what Robin was saying and understood her situation.

"Of course! You have just gotten to town and probably have a lot of quick adjustments to make. I don't suppose you've had a chance to make any plans for Christmas. Do you have family coming to visit?"

"We are still a little unsettled as yet. No, no family coming this year. It's just Martin and me," Robin explained politely. "And we have no firm plans for Christmas."

"In that case," suggested Edna, "How about joining Fred and me at our house for Christmas dinner?"

"Oh, Edna, we couldn't. That would be such a last-minute imposition on you and your family."

"It would be no imposition at all," assured Edna. "It would actually be sort of a rescue for us."

"A rescue?"

Edna laughed. "You see my sister and her family were going to join us but just this afternoon something came up and they have had to cancel. So, we'll be alone, too."

"But..."

"Alone with a lot of food. You see, I have already bought just about everything for a big Christmas dinner. I've already made some of the pies. Pies are kind of a tradition with us. But without my sister's family we can't possibly eat everything. We'll just have to throw away so much. It would be such a waste. So, you see you could help rescue our Christmas dinner if you would join us."

"But..."

"We'd love to have you. It would be our pleasure."

"Oh, my! In that case, how can I refuse such a nice invitation? We would love to come. Thank you so much. We'll look forward to joining you."

"I'll give you a call to let you know times and the address," beamed Edna. "I'm looking forward to getting to know you folks. Oh, excuse me I have to speak to Virginia over there." And Edna turned and went off to catch up to Virginia.

"Yes," agreed Mr. Spencer after making Martin's acquaintance on the other side of the room, "your Alma Mater is a very good school. Accounting you say?"

"Yes Sir. My wife and I have just come to town. You may be aware she will be teaching here at the start of the next term."

"And where will you be working?"

"I wish I knew," laughed Martin. "Actually, I need to find something in the area now that we're here. It's not particularly a good time of year to find a job so I've got my work cut out for me. Doing some internet searches. I'm sure things will look more encouraging after the holidays."

"Martin, give my Controller a call next week," directed Mr. Spencer as he pulled one of his business cards from a shirt pocket. "He recently had an accountant leave the company and is looking for a replacement. Ask him for an appointment to interview. You can tell him I sent you." He wrote the Controller's name and direct phone extension on the back of the card before handing it to Martin.

As the party progressed Martin and Robin continued to circulate about the room meeting more and more people and enjoying the light refreshments. But the time came when it was time to head back to their apartment.

"What a nice bunch of people," said Robin as she wrapped both arms tighter around Martin's arm while they walked home from the party later that night. "And we got an invitation to join the Goforths for Christmas dinner in their home."

"Her husband's the music teacher, isn't he? The couple whose sister had to back out of her visit for some last-minute reason?"

"Yes. But how nice to invite us."

"And on top of that," smiled Martin broadly, "Mr. Spencer, suggested I make an appointment to come see his Controller next week. His company is trying to replace an accountant who left a short time ago. Can you believe it?"

"Mr. Spencer?"

"Yeah, the English teacher's husband."

"Oh! Right."

"Martin?" said Robin after they had quietly walked on a little further.

"Yes?"

"I would like to go to church on Christmas Eve."

"But we haven't been to a church. We don't belong to any around here."

"I don't think that will make one bit of difference—especially on Christmas Eve."

They walked on a little farther in silence again. Martin seemed to be mulling over something in is head.

"That's a great idea," he said finally. "OK. Which church?"

"I'd like to go to that small rustic church we saw out there in the woods. We could walk to it easily enough so we can save gas money for the car."

"Then let's do it, Robin. You were exactly right when you said this would be a Christmas we will always remember. I, for one, will never forget it."

ॐ

"Well done," complimented Shanice, "Your story sounds like it could be based on a real-life experience."

"I guess everyone has some rough spots when they start out. It just seemed to come to mind for some reason."

"OK, it's my turn again. Let me see. I think that home over there looks cozy and warm inside. I imagine that a real holiday spirit has taken over the two children that live there. Let's take a peek.

IV

"So what do you do with two excited children when Christmas is just around the corner," asked Margaret?

"Listen," answered Shanice.

ॐ

"Mom, when can we put up the Christmas tree?" asked Shane.

"We have to wait for your father," answered his mother. "Maybe we can all go and pick one out together after he gets home. But right now, we're making cookies so pay attention to what you're doing."

"Shane, stop! It's my turn to put the sprinkles on," yelled his little sister.

"It is not, Jasmine. You did two batches last time so it's still my turn. Otherwise, we won't be even."

"Both of you settle down," instructed Mom. "Look! You're making a grand mess there. There will be plenty for both of you to do but one at a time."

"But it's no fair 'cause…"

"Enough. Jasmine, you come over here and help me roll this dough into little balls to go onto the cookie sheet. Shane, you go ahead and sprinkle those that are ready to go into the oven."

"When can we go see Santa Claus?" Jasmine wanted to know.

"Yeah?" jumped in Shane. "Are his elves around here watching us right now?"

"They sure are so you both better be on your best behavior," said Mom.

"Where are they?" asked Jasmine, "I don't see them."

"You can't see them," explained Shane irritably, "they are magical and they stay invisible but they tell Santa about everything you do."

"And you, too."

"Yeah, and me too. That's why I'm being extra good."

"Is that how Santa knows what presents to bring us?" asked Jasmine, "because the elves tell him?"

"Oh," explained Mom, "I'm sure that must be one way. But Santa also reads the list in the letter you write to him."

"Oh, no! A letter," panicked Shane. "I haven't written a letter yet."

"Me either," shouted Jasmine, getting worked up. "Is it too late? Will it get to the North Pole in time?"

"Maybe we can just send Santa an email instead," suggested Shane. "Or better yet a text."

"No," interrupted Mom, "Santa likes to get real letters. It helps him get to know children a little better from their handwriting. I think, if you get started writing one today there is still time for it to reach him before he leaves on his sleigh."

"Yeah!" yelled Shane. "Mom, can you finish up the cookies by yourself so I can go write my letter?"

"Me, too?" asked Jasmine.

"Well, I guess I can manage the rest of this baking by myself," smiled Mom. "You go start writing. We'll ask Dad to mail them on his way to work tomorrow."

"Mom, my pencil isn't sharp." "Mom, I messed up, so I need a new sheet of paper." "Mom, Shane keeps looking at my letter so he can copy it." "How do you spell Claus?" "What is the date so I can put it on my letter?" "Do you know how to address the envelope?" "Should I say I've been good all year before I ask for a present?" "Do I have to fit it all on just one page?" were some of the questions that Mom fielded as the kids ran in and out of the kitchen every few minutes the whole time they were writing their letters.

"Whew!" sighed Mom, eventually. "They sure are excited," she thought to herself, "but I don't know how much of this excitement I can handle. At least the cookies are done. Next, I have to start on this kitchen while the last of these cookies cool. What a mess!"

"OK, I'm done," announced Jasmine running into the kitchen once again. "Here. I folded my letter and put some tape on it so you won't need an envelope to mail it. She tossed it on the table. "Wow, Mom, that's a lot of cookies."

"I'm done too," echoed Shane as he came skidding into the kitchen. He threw his letter on top of his sister's. "Oh, yeah, Mom, that is a huge pile of cookies," agreed Shane. "Are we going to eat them all?"

"I think there are too many for us to eat them all. What do you think we should do with some of them?" asked Mom.

"Well, Gramma's coming, isn't she? We could give her some."

"That would be nice, but I think Gramma will probably bring even more cookies with her."

"We should share them with other people," suggested Jasmine.

"Now that's a good idea. Who should we share them with?"

"Umm, we could give some to the mailman."

"Yeah, and to the newspaper lady."

"And how about the garbage man."

"We'd need three for him because there are three garbage people," explained Jasmine

"I know," said Shane excitedly, "let's give some to that old man who lives all by himself down the street."

"Great ideas," said Mom. "But for right now let's start with just one. The mail and newspaper have already come today, and the garbage doesn't get picked up for four more days. So, you two get out one of the paper plates and you can help me fix it up with cookies."

"Which paper plates?"

"The ones that say 'Merry Christmas' on them."

"I'll get it," yelled Jasmine as she ran to the cupboard to find it.

"No, I will," insisted Shane and he took off after his sister.

"I said it first."

"But I should be the one to get it."

"Woah," said Mom in a loud voice. "You two come back in here. I'll get the plate. You each pick out three or four cookies to put on it for the man down the street."

Mom quickly retrieved the right plate and the kids each selected cookies to go on it (though not without some disagreement about who was the first one to choose which type of cookie). Mom covered the filled plate with plastic wrap and tied it with a big bow. "There," she proclaimed, "ready for delivery. The two of you get your coats on and you can walk it over to 'that old man down the street'. His name is Mr. Withers. Don't go inside his house. Just hand them to him on the porch. Be polite and tell him Merry Christmas. Then come straight home."

"OK, Mom," said the kids together.

"I get to carry the plate," yelled Shane.

"No. I do," argued Jasmine.

"No arguing," scolded Mom. "Let Shane carry it this time since he's the oldest."

"But Mom...!"

"End of discussion. Now get going."

The delivery only took a few minutes, and the kids noticed their dad's car in front of their house as they were walking back home. "Dad's home," they squealed, and they rushed into the house to find their father.

"Dad, can we get a Christmas tree tonight?"

"I guess so. But let's wait until after supper. We'll have to wait until tomorrow, though, to set it up and decorate it."

All through supper there was a lively discussion that kept Mom and Dad on their toes.

"How can reindeer fly?"

"Does Santa really give a lump of coal to children who don't behave?"

"Frosty can't really talk, can he? He's just a snowman."

"Can we touch the Elf-on-the-shelf yet?"

"I'm going to get more presents than you because my stocking is bigger than yours."

"Mom, we have to save some of those cookies to put out for Santa."

"How does he fit down the chimney since he's so fat?"

"I don't get how he can get back up the chimney."

"Does Rudolf's nose really light up? There was a show about Rudolf on TV."

And the excitement was non-stop. The kids had to be reminded often to keep eating instead of talking so much. By the time desert was served Mom and Dad looked at each other and just wagged their heads but smiled remembering what it was like to be a kid at Christmas time.

"Dad, will you read us a story when we get home with the tree?"

"Tell you what," answered Dad. "When you're both ready for bed I'll read you a story but not until after you each read one out loud to me and mom."

"Which story should we read?"

"I don't care. You each pick out one of those Christmas books that you get every year from your aunt."

"Dad," said Jasmine, "we made cookies today and we delivered a plate of them to that old man. His name is Mr. Withers."

"I know. That was a very nice thing to do," said Dad. "Was he surprised to get them?"

"Yes, I think so," answered Shane. "He said thank you very much and his eyes started to cry a little. But he smiled, too, and said Merry Christmas."

"Well, that's great. Good job, you two. I'm sure you made him happy."

"Dad," continued Shane.

"Yes, Shane, what is it?"

"Mr. Withers was wearing his coat."

"So?"

"He was in his house."

"Maybe he was getting ready to go out."

"No, he was wearing it in his house. He didn't go out after we left."

"Maybe it was a sweater or a heavy shirt."

"No, Dad. He was wearing his heavy outdoor coat inside his house—kind of like he was cold or something. He wasn't getting ready to go anywhere. He was just staying home."

"Hmm," thought Dad out loud, "that is a little strange. But don't worry about it. Let me think about it a little. We don't want to say or do anything that will embarrass him. Now go get bundled up so we can go pick out a tree. It's cold outside tonight." And the two took off on a run.

"Those two are really worked up," Mom told Dad. "I've never seen anyone as excited about this season as they are."

"They're still at the right age."

"Yeah," said Mom almost dreamily. "One of these days they'll be too old, and the excitement will be toned way down. One of these days."

"You're right," consoled Dad. "But for this year—well, I guess that's what it's all for—the kids. And I'm glad to see them so happy."

ಞ

"What a nice story, Shanice," gushed Margaret. "I think you just captured the whole spirit of the holiday. It's what everyone thinks about when they see a little village like this one."

"Thank you, Margaret. I know what you mean but I think this holiday has a lot of different faces. We don't always, if ever, see some or any of them because they often stay hidden behind the closed doors of the lights and trappings and hustle and bustle of the season. And inside pretty houses with glowing yellow windows."

"And sometimes we just don't look for them or we choose not to see them," added Margaret.

"Exactly." Shanice seemed to slip into a trance for just a second as if she was thinking. Then changed the mood by suggesting, "I think we need another pitcher of family recipe eggnog. How about it?"

"What? Oh, uh, do you really think we should?"

"Why not? Why don't I go and mix one up while you imagine another family in the village? It'll be your turn for a story when I get back."

"Well, I, uh, umm, Shanice, I, uh," stammered Margaret. And then she tossed her head back, and with a laugh and the wave of her hand declared, "Oh, why not indeed? Of course, we need another pitcher. Go. Go get started," she admonished, "Let me put my thinking cap on."

"That nice looking house over there," Margaret said pointing when Shanice reentered the room carrying a tray with a full pitcher of eggnog and a fresh plate of cookies. "That house looks like its special. I see a fireplace burning through the front windows and a couple of folks are sitting near it. Let's see what might be going on inside."

Margaret helped herself to a cookie and held out her glass for Shanice to fill.

V

The two ladies settled in and peered into the glowing windows of Grandma's house. Let's see how Grandma and Grandpa are getting ready for Christmas.

☙

"Here we are, Father," said Grandma. "We've grown into a couple of old fogies keeping warm by the fireplace before we get ready for bed." She laughed.

"Ha-ha-ha," snorted Grampa. "You're right, Mother. Look at us. It's not quite eight o'clock and neither one of us can stay awake much longer."

"It's amazing how age treats a person," offered Grandma. "Remember when we were a couple of young sprouts. We had the world by the tail, and nothing was going to slow us down."

"I remember, Mother. And then children came along. That kind of changed the way we looked at things a little. It caused more than a few changes in our lifestyle."

"You're right. But, in hindsight, I wouldn't have had it any other way. It was a challenge at times and there didn't seem to be enough hours in a day trying to keep up with some of their antics. But all in all, they were great kids."

"They ARE great kids," corrected Grampa. "Well, they're not kids anymore but I guess they'll always be *our* kids. Like you said, there were times, though, when they didn't seem so great."

"Yeah, growing up can be tough. But they all made it and they all turned out to be good parents."

"Well, they had a good teacher and a good role model. You did a fine job with them, Mother."

"Achh! Thank you. But I'm glad the kids can't see us now."

"Why?" asked Grandpa surprised.

"Well, our generation isn't exactly like theirs. They may not want to be seen hanging out with old folks. We'd probably be a real drag on them." Then she chuckled at what she had just said. "A drag. That's a word from a past generation. I wonder if young people still say it."

"Now, Mother, I think you're being a little extreme. Of course, they'd like to visit. They are our family, after all."

"I know. I'm just joking a little. But still, they're so young and vivacious and we're so old and sluggish now. They've got their own families and their own interests."

"I think you're feeling a little melancholy Mother, or maybe a little lonesome because it's Christmas time. It's not like what you were used to at Christmas for so many years. Back when there were lots of little voices and laughter and noise and good cheer around the house."

"I suppose you're right. It sure would be nice to have the grandkids here for Christmas, wouldn't it?"

"Yes, it would. Have you suggested that to any of the kids?" asked Grandpa.

"My yes, I have, but they all live so far away. It is very difficult to disrupt a whole family to travel so far for a stay of only a day or two. Besides, all of them agree that their children deserve to open their presents in their own home on Christmas day and then stay there to play with them instead of having to put them right away while they leave on a trip to Grandma's."

"Yes, that's a good tradition. They got that from you."

"Yes, they did. It's what we used to do, and it worked fine," affirmed Grandma.

"We could go visit them for Christmas if we were invited," suggested Grampa.

"I'm too old for that, Father. Traveling that far isn't fun anymore, either by driving or flying. All the hassle now days. And then the freakishness of the weather this time of year. No thanks."

"Well, I'm sure we'll see the grandkids later in the year if the families stop by here on their way to or from their vacation. That is if their vacation takes them in this direction."

"We've been alone for Christmas for several years now so I should be used to it," admitted Grandma. "But it's still hard."

"What? I'm not enough excitement for you at Christmas?" joked Grampa.

"Of course, you are, dear. You know what I mean. I just wish I was still up to the cooking and some of the old traditions that would make it feel more like Christmas."

"We've got the tree."

"Yes. Thank you for continuing to decorate every year. I know it's a lot of work for you," cooed Grandma.

"Well, I cut way back this year, I'm afraid. That tree is pretty puny compared to what we used to have. It's the only sprucing up I did inside. And I only got a few simple outside decorations up. But no one ever comes by to see any of them anyway. The trimmings go up and then they come down and no one cares. No one even sings carols anymore. If we want music we can just turn on the TV and listen to the carols that the seasonal channel plays all day long. I think they even show a collage of nice Christmas scenes and decorations while the tunes are playing. It's all kind of plastic or artificial. So impersonal. What has Christmas become, anyway?"

"I care," said Grandma.

"What?"

"I care."

"You do?"

"Yes, I do. I probably just never say so. I'm sorry. I really do appreciate the effort you put into it every year."

"Why, thank you, but if that is a sneaky way to get me to do more next year, it's not going to work. Like you said, I'm just not up to it all anymore," explained Grampa.

"No, I'm not being sneaky. I understand."

Grampa sat quietly for a few minutes. Then, as if the thought just occurred to him he asked, "What about cooking?"

"Cooking?"

"Yes, what are you planning to do about Christmas dinner?"

"Me?"

"Yes, you. Who else?"

"How about you?" asked Grandma. "Why don't you take a shot at cooking dinner this year?"

"I can do that," answered Grampa, "if you want a hot dog and baked beans this year."

"That's a far cry from roast turkey, chestnut dressing, candied sweet potatoes, green bean casserole, cranberry sauce and pumpkin pie," said Grandma thoughtfully. Then she laughed.

"Take your choice. Hot dogs or someone else cooks."

"Well, I'm sorry but I just can't do it anymore," answered Grandma sadly.

"I know. I'm teasing. I understand, too. So, what other options do we have?"

"We could go out to a restaurant. But, no, it's too late to make a reservation for Christmas day. Besides the crowds are so large and the traffic so heavy and the portions so big and the price is outlandish."

"So? Will it be hot dogs?" Grandpa asked again in a teasing voice.

Grandma thought quietly for a while. "Let's go to the church. They're serving a full Christmas dinner to anyone who shows up for the price of a free will donation."

"Church, huh?" And Grampa turned and stared into the embers in the fireplace. "You know, Mother," he finally said in a strong firm voice, "we're old, that's true. But look at us. We're acting old."

"Acting old. What do you mean by that?"

"I mean it's like we've given up. It's like life is almost over for us and we're just sitting around waiting to die. We don't do anything anymore. It's almost as if some rule says you have to stop being active when you get old."

"Now, Father, you're getting pretty worked up."

"I suppose I am. But why should we just quit. Why shouldn't we go out and celebrate a life of our own. We're not tied down to children or debt or a rocking chair. At least I'm not and in spite of what you might think sometimes, you're really not either. Why don't we turn over a new leaf and do wild and crazy things, again?"

"Father!" scoffed Grandma loudly and in an equally firm voice. But he knew she was not scolding. It was her way of pausing the conversation a minute to think it over.

"Of course," Grampa continued, "Our wild and crazy things would be much tamer and slower than they would have been in the past. They wouldn't have to take a lot of energy or strength or athleticism."

"I should hope not."

"Look," offered Grampa in conclusion, "we both have aches and pains. Everyone our age does. But in spite of that we both have reasonably good health. We're mobile and not handicapped and we have enough energy and stamina to get out of these chairs for a few hours every day."

"Yes, you're right. OK, count me in. But what does all that have to do with going to church for Christmas dinner?"

"I think church for dinner is a great idea. Let's do it. But let's start our new life right off the bat this way: Let's get involved and help in some way. Let's not just go eat dinner at the church. Let's volunteer to help serve it. It will get us out of the house. It will help us socialize a little. It will make things all feel more like Christmas should feel. And it will just be a good and right thing to do."

Grandma sighed. Then she was silent again for a minute or two while she sat and stared at Grampa. Then she said, "That is a great idea, Father. I'll phone the church first thing in the morning and ask what we can do to help. This *is* going to be a really good Christmas."

"It is for sure," agreed Grampa. "Hey, would you like a cup of hot chocolate?"

"No. That's too much caffeine this close to bedtime."

&

"Ha-ha-ha, too much caffeine," laughed Shanice. "Maybe they would like some eggnog instead." And she laughed some more as she raised her glass again.

"You looked like you were enjoying yours during my story," teased Margaret. "That hardly seems fair," she chuckled, "so now it's your turn while I work on my glass."

"Sounds good to me," agreed Shanice. "Umm, look at that house over there. There's another side to the holiday season, and I can imagine that it's coming to light in that home."

VI

"Christmas means different things to different people," explained Shanice, "but, I think most of us forget or never think that some folks in a neighborhood have another opinion about it all. Listen as these young men are about to see another point of view."

≈

"Hi, Stephan," said Benny as he opened the front door to welcome his fourth-grade classmate and friend. "C'mon in. Glad your mom let you come over to play. Just throw your coat on the chair over there."

"Yeah. No school for a while." said Stephan as he stopped for a moment and looked around the room. "Let's go look at your Christmas tree."

"We don't have one," said Benny.

"When are you going to get one? It's almost Christmas."

"I know. We don't have Christmas trees."

"What do you mean?"

"We don't ever get a Christmas tree."

"What? Why not?" asked Stephan surprised.

"Because we're Jewish," explained Benny.

"So?"

"So, Christmas trees are a decoration that helps celebrate Christmas."

"Yeah. So why don't you get one?"

"Because we don't celebrate Christmas. We celebrate Hanukkah."

"I don't get it," confessed Stephan. "What's Hanukkah?"

"It's what we celebrate instead of Christmas."

"Maybe I can help explain," interrupted Benny's mom, Edith. When she had heard the word Hanukkah her ears perked up and she thought she had better eaves drop a bit. It was a chance to see just how much Benny really understood about the holiday and it was a chance to teach his non-Jewish friend a little about their religion. She walked into the room and sat down near the boys.

"Christmas is a Christian holiday," she began. "Jewish people believe in Judaism not Christianity. Do you understand?"

"I guess so," said Stephan, "but I'm not sure."

"Well, Christianity is a religion. People who are Christian believe in Jesus."

"Judaism is a religion, too," chimed in Benny quickly.

"That's right," confirmed his mother in a quiet manner, "but Jewish people don't' believe in Jesus in the same way Christians do. Jewish people think Jesus was a great prophet or a teacher or a Rabbi, but we don't believe he is the Messiah. Do you know what that means?"

"Uh, not really," confessed Stephan. He was not sure if pleading ignorance would make him look stupid or make Benny's mom angry.

"Messiah means Savior like in saving the world," explained Edith.

"Oh," replied Stephan still uncertain but trying to be polite.

"So, we don't celebrate Jesus' birthday like the Christians do at Christmas."

"That's weird," said Stephan confused. Edith laughed lightly.

"It is not," protested Benny.

"Then why do you call Christmas Hanukkah?"

"We don't. Hanukkah is a different and separate celebration," answered Edith gently. "It is not Christmas. It's not even on the same day as Christmas. But it does come very close to Christmas—around the same time but at a different time each year. Our Hanukkah is already over this year. It was before Christmas this time. It's also called the Festival of Lights."

"Then what do you celebrate?"

"Well," began Edith, "can you explain it to him, Benny?" she asked.

"Hanukkah celebrates when they built a new temple in the old days."

"What?"

"Yeah. There was a long war and stuff and when it was over a temple that got wrecked was fixed back up."

"What's a temple?"

"It's like a church that you go to."

"That's weird," repeated Stephan. "Do you get presents?"

"We get presents for eight days."

"Eight?"

"Yep. Each day during the celebration."

"So, Hanukkah lasts for eight days?"

"Yep."

"And Santa Claus comes to your house eight times every year?"

"No, we don't believe in Santa Claus."

"Then who gives you presents?"

"Hanukkah does last for eight days", interrupted Benny's mother. "Presents for the children come from parents, grandparents, aunts and uncles and a lot of different relatives. But the most important thing about Hanukkah is not the presents."

"It's not?"

"No," jumped in Benny, "Each day when the sun goes down, we light a candle and say a prayer. Sometimes we read stuff from the Torah and talk about the olden war and Jerusalem and the temple and about how the Jews were slaves and all kinds of stuff like that."

"The Torah? What's the Torah?"

"It's kinda like your Bible."

"It's the first five books of the Old Testament or The Jewish Bible," added Edith. "It's also called the Pentateuch."

"Oh."

"And we play games like with the dreidel," said Benny.

"What's a dray-dull?" asked Stephan trying to pronounce what he heard Benny say.

"It's this top," said Benny pulling one out of a drawer and showing it to Stephan. "It has four sides, and you spin it. When you play you try to win a 'pot of *Gelt*'. It's not really gold. It's mostly round pieces of chocolate candy wrapped up in a gold-colored paper."

"So, do you have a big turkey dinner every night?"

"No. We do get to have special things to eat, though—like *latkes*. Those are special potato pancakes. And we get to have *sufganiyot*. Those are jam-filled donuts."

Stephan thought for a few quiet minutes and then asked, "Where are all your decorations if you're having a celebration?"

"We have the Menorah," bragged Benny.

"What's that?"

"It's this candelabra."

"What's a candelabra?"

"It's something that holds candles. A candle holder with eight candles in it. The ninth candle—the one in the middle—is used to light the other candles. When we say that prayer each night, we light one candle. We light one each night during Hanukkah," explained Edith.

"But, what about Christmas?" puzzled Stephan. "We hang up stockings and get lots of presents all at the same time on Christmas day and do lots of other things."

"Yeah," sighed Benny a little dreamily. "That must be great. I think I would really like your way."

"And I think I really like Hanukkah," thought Stephan out loud, "Special pancakes and jelly-donuts and presents every day for eight days. That must be great!"

"As if that's all there was to it," sighed Edith quietly. "You boys go find something to play with. Why don't you show Stephan how the dreidel works, Benny?"

And the boys headed off to another room on a dead run.

৯

"Good story, Shanice," said Margaret when there was a long pause indicating that the image had ended. "I guess we're often guilty of forgetting that maybe everyone doesn't see Christmas the same way. But isn't there another group that we should include?"

"Another group? Which one?" asked Shanice.

"I think they celebrate Kwanzaa."

"Oh, right. But that's not a religious group or a religious celebration. As a matter of fact, it is not considered to be a substitute for Christmas. It's a weeklong celebration starting on the day after Christmas day."

"What is Kwanzaa, exactly. It's relatively new, isn't it?"

"Yes," explained Shanice, "it's only been around since 1966 and the intention is to celebrate culture rather than religion or politics. It's primarily an African American holiday and celebrates seven principles of black or African culture."

"So, it doesn't really conflict with Christmas or Hanukkah. Interesting."

"So, now what do you think of my little neighborhood?" asked Shanice.

"Beautiful," reiterated Margaret, "I love it."

"So do I," confirmed Shanice. "But it can be so many different things whether you want it to or not. Mostly I like to, oh, look at it superficially, I guess you could say. I mean, I like to just see and feel the beautiful and joyful side of Christmas. The feel-good side."

"But some of these stories that you create?"

"Yeah, once in a while, when I have time to sit a little longer than usual and consider things a little more deeply, I start to imagine what it's like on the less glitzy side of the holiday—you know, real life. I guess it helps keep me grounded."

"I suppose that can be a good thing."

"I think so. But it can be sad and disheartening sometimes, too. We've seen a little of that already in our stories tonight. For some reason I feel like there may be another one or two coming. I don't know," Shanice paused for a few seconds.

"So, what do you think?" she asked coming back into the moment. "Want to continue or take a break first? Or have you just had enough and you're ready to quit?"

"Shanice," said Margaret strongly, "I love your little village and I have thoroughly enjoyed our trip through it so far—building by building. And, no, that's not the eggnog talking. I could use a potty break, though, so let's put it on hold for a few minutes and then let's keep going."

"I'm with you," said Shanice. "I'll check on the guys to be sure they're not ready to give up on their game yet."

"Great! I think it's my turn to visualize a scenario when we come back."

A few minutes later as she reentered the room, Margaret said loudly, "OK. Let's see," she pondered a minute while studying the little buildings. "All the lights seem to be on in the school building. There must be something big going on in there. Let's take a look."

VII

Margaret introduced her story by saying, "while it's normally closed for maintenance during the winter break, this year the school is open and active for a day as it tries on a brand-new program for the kids and for the community. Let's watch how it all unfolds."

॰

"Uh Oh," said Millie Johnson to herself though in a voice loud enough for her approaching visitor to hear, "here comes the boss so we better be on our toes." And she laughed as she waited while Colleen continued the short walk over to her.

"Good morning. You're here early," greeted Millie.

"No earlier than you and the others. Someone has to make the rounds, you know—to be sure we're ready to pull this thing off today."

"I guess that's what you do when you're the President of the Parent/Teacher Organization," said Millie. "It's going to be busy all day with lots of activity and energy. What a great idea you and the board had."

"Thank you, Millie," said Colleen, "we'll see how good our plan turned out to be when we get to the end of the day. It sure has been a lot of work bringing it together."

"It can't fail," assured Millie. "Look what you're doing. You are giving all the kids something creative to do for a whole day during their holiday break—keeping them occupied, keeping them from getting bored. They also get a free lunch, a sports event, a concert and a shopping spree."

"Whew! It makes me tired thinking about it when you put it that way. By-the-way, Mrs. Art Teacher, thank you again for volunteering your time to help the kids 'create', as you say."

"You're quite welcome. It'll be fun, especially with all these materials Mrs. Mapleton donated from her craft store. Look at this assortment of beads, styrofoam balls and shapes, paints, kits, patterns and, well, just look at it all."

"Isn't it great? But let me move on so you can finish sorting all this out. Kids are going to start showing up in a few minutes. Good luck."

With that Colleen walked out of the large room that was the Art Lab and headed down the hallway. Millie continued to arrange various craft materials by type of art and by designated spots in the room. She was expecting a large number of kids this morning whether they were art students or not. Before she had completely finished her sorting the first few started showing up.

After a good sized group had accumulated, she gathered them together, as she would continue to do with new groups throughout the morning, and explained, "The idea is to make something appropriate to the season and then either take it along home with you or take it to the gym later this afternoon and put it out on a table and up for sale. All the money we make from everything that's going on today will go to the school as part of its fundraiser. So do a good job. You can pretty much work in any medium you want to. Pottery, statuary, and ceramic creations will have to wait until another show before they can be sold because it will take time to fire them in the kiln. I'll just roam the area and help anyone who needs it or asks for it. Have fun."

"How d'ya like this jewelry, Mrs. Johnson?" asked Rita a little later.

"Very pretty, Rita," answered Millie. "Hmm, I suggest that you mix in a variety of different size beads. Try it and see what you think. I'll bet you have time to make several pieces to take to the sale."

"C'mere, Mrs. Johnson," called Byron, "Uh, please. This dumb snowman just doesn't fit right. I can't get him t' look 'sactly like he should when I try t' paint him. I need help."

"Oh, no!" wailed Susan, "my shepherd boy just slumped down and bent in half. Stupid clay! Do I have it too soft, Mrs. Johnson? How do I get this figure to stay straight up anyway?"

"How'cha like these Styrofoam tree ornaments, Mrs. Johnson?"

"Very nice, Shannon. Do a careful job painting them."

At that point a boy across the room started waving his arms calling out to the teacher.

"Yes, what is it?" asked Millie as she walked over to him. "You're not in any of my classes but I saw you in the hall the other day. Your History teacher told me your name is Xavier. Right?"

"Jus' call me 'X'. That's, you know, cool."

"OK, X, can I help you with something?"

"Yeah, my mom wants a cup. How d'ya make a cup? Is dis da stuff you use? You know da stuff you call clay"

"Yes," explained Millie. "That's clay that you have on the table in front of you. First you have to work with the clay to get it to the right consistency. Here like this," and she picked up a chunk that was lying beside the boy and showed him how to go about it. She spent a lot of time walking him through the whole process and when she got to the potter's wheel, his interest seemed to increase. He perked up and appeared to enjoy what he was doing.

"OK, X," she said finally, "you finish it yourself now. I have to go help Gerald." And off walked Millie leaving X on his own. He didn't notice she had gone. He just kept right on working.

And so, the morning progressed until it was time for a hot dog lunch prepared, served and cleaned up by volunteer PTO dads. It was all done with ingredients donated by the butcher and the grocer and the baker in town.

"May I have a third hot dog and another piece of cake?" asked Ronnie. The cafeteria had filled quickly with kids. Colleen was on hand to see how it was all going (and to quickly snarf down a hot dog before she had to move along to another station).

"The basketball game will begin in twenty minutes," Colleen announced. "If you don't want to attend you may continue to work on your crafts." Taking her bottle of water with her she headed for the gym.

"Thanks, again, coach, for moving your game up to early afternoon today. I hope Ratchfield wasn't too upset about rescheduling it," she said a few minutes later on the court sideline.

"You're welcome," replied the varsity coach as he watched his team go through their warm-up drills at one end of the floor. "Coach Riley was quite happy to play earlier in the day, especially after I explained what we're trying to do here today. If this is successful, maybe we can turn it into an annual event and put it in the year's schedule early like this."

"Not a bad idea," replied Colleen. "I hope it doesn't distract your boys from playing their best."

"Not a chance. They're all kind of excited about the whole thing. Some of them spent an hour before practice this morning in the craft area. And don't worry, the team will set up your tables in the gym here as soon as the game is over. You should be good-to-go by midafternoon."

Then, before Colleen turned to leave, the coach added, "It looks like we're going to have a larger than usual crowd for the game today because of your plan. Yes sir, maybe we should schedule something like this more often." Then spotting a teaching moment on the other side of the court, the coach took off across the floor. Colleen grinned broadly and headed off down another corridor to oversee the final preparations being made there for the craft sale.

Later after the basketball game had ended and the craft sale had started, the "boss lady" took a short breather. "Look at this crowd," said Colleen to Millie as she leaned inconspicuously against a back wall and watched the shopping activity going on in the gym.

"Yeah, I can't believe it. Not only have the kids stayed around to buy and sell but their parents have turned out in a big way," said Millie.

"And besides that, some of the parents and relatives that were spectators from the visiting Ratchfield team have stayed and are shopping, too," smiled Colleen.

"Amazing! And there are some very nice things to buy. The kids did a wonderful job on their crafts. They've turned out some lovely holiday art," said Millie.

"Hi, Mrs. Johnson," interrupted Shirel. "Y'know that tree ornament I made? The one I wanted t' keep? The one the other kids said I should sell?" she asked excitedly.

"Yes, Shirel," answered Millie, "You did a very nice job on it. It was beautiful."

"Well, it got sold," gushed the girl, "and it was sold for a lot of money. Want to know who bought it?"

"Congratulations. I'm very happy for you that it got sold, Shirel. Yes, who bought it?"

"My uncle," said Shirel almost screaming with delight, "and then y'know what? He gave it to me t' hang on our tree at home. Isn't that crazy?"

"Yeah, crazy," agreed Millie but it was too late for Shirel to hear because she was already skipping happily across the room to browse another table. Colleen and Millie looked at each other and laughed.

"Well, I must go see how our silent auction is going," decided Colleen. "We had some really great prizes to bid on."

"I know," said Millie, "I'm excited to see who won that cruise or who bought those concert tickets or that Willie Mays baseball card or that diamond brooch or, well, any of those great items that your board got donated. Wish I could afford something," and she laughed.

"Me too," confided Colleen, and she joined in the laugh as she headed off.

Then late into the afternoon, after the sale was over, the school choir presented the last event of the day. When the final musical note had sounded and as the applause faded but before anyone had a chance to leave their seats, Colleen stepped out onto the stage.

"Thank you, Mr. Goforth, and each member of your school choir," she said. She spoke into the microphone to a full auditorium. "What a great holiday concert and sing-along and what a great way to end this day."

"I can think of only one better way to wrap up this long but perfect day and that is to announce the preliminary results of our fund raising. There may be a few more dollars coming in but to this point we have raised a lot of money. That is all thanks to everyone who donated to and participated in today's activities.

"And the PTO has decided that we will use all the money we raised to give each and every teacher and staff member in this school a holiday bonus."

There followed a loud and raucous cheer which brought a busy day to a happy end.

ঞ

"What a great vision, Margaret," exclaimed Shanice. "I would never have imagined something like that going on in the school building. Nice!"

"Thank you," said Margaret a little slyly. "But now, if you think that was good, it's your turn to do better."

"That sounds like a challenge," said Shanice. She chuckled. "Let's see now. Ah, yes, there is a house that I would like to explore. I know. I'm going to continue the story I started earlier."

"Is that allowed? Which one? Oh, and by-the-way, I didn't mean this as a challenge. Maybe that was finally the eggnog speaking."

"Never mind," smiled Shanice anxious to get into her story. "Look over here through these windows with me," she said pointing to a less brightly lit house, "and you will quickly remember which earlier story I'm talking about. But hear me out because this may not be one of those kinds of stories anyone likes to hear, especially during the Christmas season."

VIII

"Can you visualize the man and woman on the front porch of that darkened house?" asked Shanice.

"Yes."

"Well, listen in. We've met the man briefly before."

※

"Now let's be sensitive about this whole meeting," instructed Chloe having just climbed the steps to the porch, "We don't know anything about his circumstances, and we can't assume there is any problem."

"Yeah, yeah, yeah, I know, sis."

"Just don't barge in like a bull-in-a-china-shop and start asking judgmental questions."

"I won't. Promise. That's why I brought you along. You're the one trained in this sort of thing—well, at least a little bit."

"Not much but, yeah, more than you are," she laughed and ragged her brother a little. "OK, ring the bell then."

But before the button got pushed, the door opened unexpectedly.

"Oh!" was the gasp that came from both sides of the door at the same time. The dour old man on the inside regained his composure first and said without emotion, "I'm sorry to frighten you. I heard voices out here and thought you were the lady from Meals on Wheels. It's a little early for her but I thought, well... may I help you?"

"Mr. Withers, my name is Earl Henderson, and this is my sister Chloe."

"Yes, I know who you are. You live down the street a bit. Before you go any further, please come inside so we don't let any more heat out through this open door."

Earl and Chloe glanced at each other briefly with a surprised look on their faces. "Let more heat out?" They quickly stepped into the vestibule and after closing the door behind them, Earl began, "Mr. Withers, my children..."

"Yes," interrupted the gaunt gentleman still speaking weakly and without a smile, "your children brought me a plate of Christmas cookies the other day. They were very polite. You cannot know how much I appreciated the cookies or the gesture. Tell them thank you for me again."

"I will, Mr. Withers. They are the reason we came to see you today."

"Please just call me Charlie," said the man. "Here, follow me into another room and we can sit down."

Though Charlie said he knew who the two were, he was naturally being cautious about this unexpected visit from semi-strangers. But as he turned to lead the way further into the house it seemed to the two visitors that the man was starting to warm to them a little though his demeanor was still very low key and he seemed sad in a way.

They noticed, as they passed through the house, that it was mostly dark and seemed to contain very few pieces of furniture. It was also chilly. The room they finally entered though, was lavishly decorated for Christmas. There was a large brightly lit tree and draped garlands and unlit candles of all sizes set in ornate trimmers and a very old, but obviously special, manger scene that consumed nearly the whole top of the coffee table.

"Please have a seat," urged Mr. Withers, "anywhere you like." He sat down in a very well broken-in recliner after his two guests were seated side by side on the couch. "I'm sorry," he said, "I have nothing that I can offer you to drink and I'm afraid I finished your children's cookies already."

"That's fine Mr... uh, Charlie," replied Chloe. "We didn't expect anything like that. We just came for a short visit. We wanted to see you."

"Well, I'm glad you came," answered the old man. "No one comes to see me anymore. 'Course, I do keep pretty much to myself nowadays."

"Charlie," barged in Earl, "we came because my children were concerned about you. They were surprised to see you wearing your coat in the house the day they brought the cookies over. They somehow sensed that something might be, well, wrong." The statement somehow had the effect of breaking through the man's guarded demeanor and he immediately felt more at ease. He began speaking a little more confidentially to his visitors.

"You have fine children, Mr. Henderson, and they are very observant. I do often wear my coat in the house. You see I do not set the thermostat very high. That's so I can save a little money on my heating bill. My coat is another layer over my shirt and sweater that helps keep me warm. I didn't mean to alarm the little ones." Mr. Withers spoke now without reservation though there was a sadness in his voice as his words came softly but steadily.

"Mr. Withers," burst in Chloe, "You just alarmed me a little. I don't want to intrude on your privacy nor to be impertinent, but I must ask if you, uh, are you, let's say, short of cash?"

"Sis!" scolded Earl. "And you warned me."

Charlie smiled very slightly without stirring in his chair. Then he explained, "Folks, I'm sorry to tell you, I am broke. I have nothing but a monthly Social

Security check to live on. And that is just barely enough to pay my few bills and for the medicine I must take. I try to keep my expenses as small as possible and cut out as much as I can. That's why I wear a coat in the house sometimes."

He paused and noticing only looks of surprise and unbelief from his visitors he continued. "I have no car. I sold that when I needed extra cash so, in a way, I might be considered homebound. The local group of the Meals on Wheels program accepts the fact that I am. I think it's their way to justify or allow me to qualify for their program. I do pay them a very small amount in return for them delivering me a hot meal every day. I don't know what I'd do without them."

Earl and Chloe were incredulous and sat motionless for another minute just staring at Charlie. "We had no idea, Charlie," began Earl, "what can..."

"Thank you, but I'm afraid you can do nothing," interrupted Charlie. "I don't want to burden you with my problems." At that point Charlie broke down and became very pensive. Then he turned away from his visitors to hide the emotions that were starting to screw up his face.

Noticing this, Chloe suggested softly, "Maybe it would help you to talk about it. Maybe it would help to get it all out in the open. It is no burden on us. Please don't think so."

Charlie sat quietly. He took a minute to straighten his face and regain his self-control. Then he turned back to the pair. In a sad soft voice he said, "You're right. I haven't explained this to anyone but maybe it's time I did. It might help me to cope a little better.

"You see, my Evelyn and I had a good life for many years. I was always lucky in business and business was good to me. We became used to success and good fortune. We became very well-to-do. Oh, we weren't rich, by any means, but we lived comfortably and saved up a very nice retirement account.

"But I was proud—and, in retrospect, stupid. I thought we could control our own destiny, so to speak. We were independent and didn't need anything from anyone. We didn't ever want any help. We bought only the minimum basic health insurance and no long-term care insurance of any kind. It just always seemed to me that our nest egg would more than cover any such need. But then, we never anticipated ever needing anything like that anyway." He paused and took a deep breath.

"But soon after I retired, Evelyn came down with a rare disease. I can't tell you what it was because I never could pronounce it. As it progressed, we reached the point where I could no longer care for her at home. She was moved to a nursing home where she received round-the-clock care. She never did recover but she lingered for years which, slowly but surely, consumed every penny we had in our savings account. At the time of her death, I had nothing left. I was penniless. So now, after never needing anyone else, I am very dependent on just about everyone else just to stay alive."

"Is there no other family?" Earl wanted to know.

"No, I'm afraid not. We lost our only child in an accident many years ago. I'm not sure that didn't play into Evelyn's condition somehow. Anyway, I am left to survive alone."

"But this house. Surely you do not need as much room anymore. It is an asset that could be sold."

"No sir," answered Charlie firmly and stubbornly, "I'm afraid not. This is our house. It has been ours for many years. There is no mortgage on it. It is all paid for. Evelyn would not want me to give it up, nor do I want to. Besides, the money I could get for it would not last long in today's economy and I would soon find myself right back in the same circumstance but without a home."

"Charley, your Christmas decorations are beautiful," said Chloe, "and there are a great number of them. Surely you spent a lot of money on them that you might have saved. Oh, please forgive me for being presumptuous."

"That's alright. I understand. Thank you, but they were not expensive because they are all artificial. Paper and plastic and all very old. They just get put away at the end of the season and brought back out again the next year. I have invested no money in them for a long time. I bring the same ones out and put them up every year in remembrance of my Evelyn. Christmas was her very favorite time of the year and she loved these decorations and this room when it glowed with its seasonal trappings.

"While she was living at the nursing home, I was able to bring her home for a day once in a while. Christmas day seemed to cheer her the most and she perked up a little in this room on that day. The decorations are for her, but I guess they help me remember, too."

"Charlie," said Chloe, "I'm very sorry. Do you get out of the house much?"

"When the weather is nice, I walk in the park a lot. I like to watch the children playing there. I say hello to some of the folks sometimes, but I don't really have any friends there."

"So, you like children?"

"I love children."

"Charlie?" said Earl impulsively, "How about coming home with me and spending a little time being a grampa to Shane and Jasmine this afternoon? They would love it and it would give their mother and me a break so we can finish getting ready for Christmas."

Charlie was quiet for a minute or two thinking seriously about Earl's offer. Finally, he looked up and said, "Tell you what. Just as soon as the lady from Meals on Wheels drops off my supper, I'll walk down to your house."

"Great!" said Earl. "I'll talk to the kids about it and let them know to expect you."

"Thank you, both, so much and Merry Christmas." Mr. Withers stood as a signal that he thought it was time for his guests to leave.

Earl and Chloe stood and left the house. Once the door closed behind them Chloe said to her brother, "The poor man. Besides having no money his biggest problem is that he's lonely."

"You're right," agreed Earl as they walked home, "and this could be an especially lonely time of year for someone like him."

"Yeah. I have an idea about how we might be able to take the edge off a little bit of that. C'mon, I've got phone calls to make."

Sometime later, when Charlie arrived at the Henderson's home and before the children could run to greet him, Chloe took his arm and ushered him to another room where she could talk to him confidentially.

"Charlie, I took the liberty to make some arrangements—if you agree with them. How would you like to come over to my pre-school center a few days a week and hang out with the children as a volunteer? You could read to them and be kind of a grandpa to them. I wouldn't be able to pay you anything, but it would get you out of the house. It would give you something to do and it would be a big help to me and the other teachers."

"Hmm," thought Charlie. Chloe patiently gave him all the time he needed to process what was a new idea to him. "Yes, I think I would like that." Then, "that would be great," he said starting to tear up a bit. "Why, I never imagined such a thing. Thank you."

"I'll get back to you with details after the holidays when school starts back up."

And at that point two rambunctious children tore into the room, grabbed onto Charlie and almost knocked him down in their excitement.

Charlie Withers laughed—maybe for the first time in a long time—a big laugh, right out loud.

☙

"Your turn," said Shanice after giving Margaret a moment to bring her emotions under control.

"How do I follow that?" she asked. "Let me think. Maybe we need to see how some of the merchants fit into this season. Yes, that's it. I think we'll go look in on Mrs. Tieg in the bakery shop."

IX

"Mrs. Tieg is a baker and descendant of German parents, and everyone knows how good German pastry is. Look, over here," said Margaret pointing to the brightly lit bakery store-front windows.

☙

"Hi, Zach." The bell on top of the door announced her presence as it did for everyone who passed through it going in either direction.

"Good afternoon, Mrs. Goforth," answered the boy behind the counter politely as the customer entered the bakery. "May I help you? Mrs. Tieg is in the back putting a new batch of bread into the oven."

"Yes, thank you but let me look around for a minute first. Looks like you're putting in a lot of extra hours here while school is out for the holidays," she said as she walked over to a display case.

"Yes, ma'am."

"I'm sure there's a lot to do this time of year."

The boy lowered his eyes a little and a sad look crossed his face as if the statement had triggered a memory or something. "Yes, ma'am."

At that point a plump middle-aged woman walked out from the back room of the shop and Zach relinquished the counter. "You can make that delivery for me now, Zach," the woman said. "Sorry to keep you waiting."

"Yes, Mrs. Tieg. I already have it packed in the car." With that Zach left the store. Mrs. Tieg did not step into his evacuated spot but came around to the front of the counter to greet her customer.

"Merry Christmas Edna," beamed the baker.

"And to you, Hazel," was the answer.

"Don't you just love this time of year?"

"I do but I can't hold a candle to your upbeat personality. I think you set the standard for joy and merriment at Christmas. It's so warm and cheery in here and it smells delicious. By the way, you look very festive in your stained apron and your face and hairnet sprinkled with flour," joked Edna and she laughed.

"Ooh," laughed Hazel as she backed away from the counters and brushed herself off a bit. "It's my baker's uniform." And she laughed too as she stepped back over to Edna. "How can I help you today?"

"Well, I need some dinner rolls. We have invited that new schoolteacher and her husband to have Christmas dinner with us."

"Oh, how nice. There are not many rolls left. If you can wait until tomorrow, I can have some nice fresh ones for you."

"Tomorrow will be fine. Actually, anytime up until Christmas eve will be good. That should give you a little more time. It looks like you are busier than usual this year."

"Ach, you mean the empty cases. *Ja*! Just look at this. I am out of *Streuselkuchen* and gingerbread. There seems to be enough *Pfeffermusse* and *Marzipan* for right now, but the *Stollen* is all gone, and a lot of folks haven't even been in to pick theirs up yet. I must get busy and bake, bake, bake." Hazel Tieg beamed a very happy and satisfied smile.

"Oh, I thought the cases were empty just because I'm so late coming in today. I thought you were just sold out of today's goods."

"Yes, that's some of it," confirmed Hazel, "but this year I had to interrupt my baking for a whole day so I could prepare and cook those birds for Mr. Smithwell. That cut into my baking so now I am still trying to catch up."

"You cooked birds for Mr. Smithwell?"

"Yes. He had some kind of big party and needed a couple dozen pheasants roasted."

"But you're a bakery not a restaurant."

"You're right but there is no place else in town that has enough ovens or big enough ones to cook that much meat all at once. It just seemed like it would be the right kind of Christmas spirit to help out where I could. It's alright. He paid me well for it."

"So, now you have to work overtime—late into the night, I suppose, to catch up on your own business."

"*Ja*, but I don't mind. It makes me happy to see other people happy. Isn't that what this time of year is supposed to be about? I'll have your dinner rolls on Christmas Eve. I know you make your own pies at Christmas but how about a special cake for your Christmas Eve dessert?"

"Oh, hello Mr. Metzger," greeted Hazel as she turned at the sound of the front door's little bell to see a man walk into the shop. "You know the butcher from next door?" she asked Edna.

"Of course. How do you do, Mr. Metzger?"

"I'm very well, thank you," answered the man. "It's nice to see you again, Mrs. Goforth."

"Here is the package, Hazel," he said as he lifted a big basket up onto the counter. "I've included some nice chicken and some hot dogs and some ground beef. That should help get them through the holidays. Oh, and there's a cold pack on the bottom to keep everything from spoiling."

"Thank you," said Hazel with a big smile. "That should make a big difference. I'm glad you could help."

"Don't mention it, Hazel," he said. "It's the least I could do."

"Well, I'll make sure it gets delivered as soon as possible but not later than Christmas Eve. Actually, the sooner the better, I think."

"Very good. I'm sorry to interrupt but I have to get back to the shop. Merry Christmas, everyone." And with that the butcher went back out the door.

"Oh," wondered Edna, "are you getting ready to do some more cooking for someone?"

"No," answered Hazel, "this basket is for Zach."

"For Zach? I noticed he is putting in a lot more hours than usual."

"Yes, Zach is a good boy and a hard worker. He is very conscientious and a very big help to me. He's trying to earn enough money to buy something for his little brother so the boy can have a Christmas present."

"What do you mean 'so the boy can have a Christmas present'?"

"Oh, I probably shouldn't be saying anything but if you can keep it to yourself."

"Of course, Hazel," interrupted Edna, "I won't say a word."

"Well, Zach's father was laid off from his job at the factory over in Chesterton and apparently the family has very little money until he can find another job. His parents have explained to Zach that there will be no Christmas this year."

"Oh, my! No, I'm sorry. Why do companies always seem to pick this time of year to let people go?"

"*Ja*, it seems so unfair. Zach understands but he knows his brother will be very disappointed."

"So, what about the basket?"

"Well, Mr. Metzger and I have decided to help them out a bit by taking them things they can use to fix meals with. I'm going to add some bread and baked goods to the basket, and we'll give it to Zach to take home with him. He doesn't know anything about it yet."

"So, you're giving them a Christmas dinner. That's so thoughtful, Hazel."

"Well, we're giving them a Christmas present. I imagine they will eat the Christmas dinner that the church in town is offering. But there are a lot of other meals to fix until a new job is found."

"I'm so sorry," said Edna, again, at a loss as to what else to say. Then she added the familiar, "Let me know if I can do anything to help. Well, I'd better be getting on back home."

Edna turned to leave but paused as she approached the front door. She turned back in toward the shop and said to the baker, "Hazel, that special cake for dessert? I'll take two. Please put the second one in the basket for Zach's family."

"Goodness, Edna, that's just wonderful. Isn't it a great time of year? Merry Christmas to you."

"Merry Christmas to you, Hazel and thank you."

With that the little bell jingled as Edna opened the door and hurried next door to purchase some additional cuts of meat and make arrangements with Mr. Metzger to include them in Zach's basket.

☙

"What a great story, Margaret. Kind of bittersweet. You are a good storyteller."

"Oh, why thank you, Shanice. You're the one who set the goal so high. So, now it's your turn and this time I do have a challenge for you. See what you can do with the, uh, oh, the fire station."

"The fire station, huh? What could be going on at the fire station?" wondered Shanice as she took a little time to imagine who was inside and what they were doing. "I've got it!" she exclaimed finally. "Let's look at this one in a little different way."

"Oh? OK. How do you mean that?"

"Well, I imagine a van in front of the station house with the Logo of the Chesterton TV station on it? Now let's follow the reporter as he enters the building to cover a party that's going on inside."

X

Shanice explained that the TV reporter was not thrilled with his Christmas assignment to report on what he considered an insignificant activity going on at an outlying firehouse. Though he grumbled a little to his crew, he put on a positive face as he unloaded his van and headed into the station.

ॐ

"Jonathan Reallygood here," he crowed into the microphone, "at a children's holiday party hosted by a local fire department. And this firehouse is decorated to the hilt for the holidays. There's garland strung between wreaths on the walls, and it wraps all the way around the room. There are balloons all over the place. There is a huge floor to ceiling tree in the middle of the room fully decorated and brightly lit. It's circled by chairs and tables that are set with all kinds of cookies and, oh, look!

There's someone roaming the room in a Smokey Bear costume serving hot chocolate.

"I'm going to try to find the Fire Chief in this large crowd. Ah, there he is. I, somehow, need to work my way through all these children to get to him.

"Here we are. I made it. Whew! Captain Larson. Excuse me, Captain Larson," persisted Jonathan trying to get the officer's attention. "Captain Larson, may I have a few minutes?"

The Fire Chief turned away from the group of children he was talking with to see who was paging him. He smiled when he noticed the man with the microphone who was wearing a shirt imprinted with the logo of the Chesterton TV station. He stepped over closer to him. The group of children dispersed quickly as they excitedly headed off in all different directions. "Yes, of course. Thank you for coming." The reporter's cameraman turned away from him and pointed his camera at the Chief.

"Can you tell our audience, Sir, what exactly is going on here tonight?"

"I would be glad to. The department decided, this year, to sponsor a holiday party for all the children in town. It's our way of sharing with them what the joy and happiness of this season is all about. There are, no doubt, a few children who, sadly, won't experience it otherwise. The children are admitted free of charge. But the cost of admission for adults is that none can come in unless they have a child with them." The Chief grinned as if he had made a little joke.

"There's a secondary benefit, too. Hopefully, people, and kids especially, will get to know that firefighters are friendly people that help when there's trouble and people won't be afraid if they ever need one of us."

"I noticed that all of your equipment is parked outside. Is it part of the party?"

"No, we hadn't planned to highlight it or let the kids climb on it this time. It's out there for a couple of reasons. First to make plenty of room in here for all the activities. Secondly, if we absolutely have to respond to an extra alarm call, we won't have to interrupt the party to get the engines moving."

"Do you anticipate having to respond to a call tonight?"

"We hope not, of course, but we have to stay ready 24/7 just in case. We do have another station ready to cover for us tonight if a more routine call does come in."

"How do you get all those vehicles back inside after the party with that tree taking up so much room?"

"After the party we'll move the tree outside for the whole community to enjoy."

"So, it looks like there is a lot going on in here," prompted the reporter, "can you tell us about it?"

"Sure. But I'm going to let our firefighters do that. Here, this is Jake," said the chief as he corralled one of the men who was walking past. "Jake, will you conduct a little tour for Jonathan and his TV audience?"

"Sure Chief. Be glad to. C'mon Jonathan let's start over here." And Jake led the way across the room to a long silver ladder that had been set up angled into the far wall. It had been tightly secured and a thick mat had been placed underneath it. A safety harness for the climber hung down from the ceiling on a strong strap.

"It's one of the games we have for the kids who are, shall we say, brave enough to try to climb it. If any of them gets all the way to the top, there's a large bell that they can ring to let everyone know they made it. Showana keeps a close eye on everyone who makes the climb."

"So, Showana, are the kids having fun on the ladder? Do many try it?" asked Jonathan.

"They sure are," she answered. "You can see the line forming to get a turn. Ask some of the kids if they're having fun."

Jonathan turned as his cameraman swung his camera around to film the kids. "How about it, son," the reporter asked a small lad as he stuck the microphone into the boy's face, "Is the ladder fun?"

"Uh, yes," the boy answered slowly and shyly not knowing exactly what was happening. "Uh, I got up to the third step."

"I got to the fifth step," broke in a little girl as she pulled the mic over in front of her. "I'm going to do it again and this time I'm going to get to the seventh step," and she ran to get back in line. Jonathan chuckled, watched the activity for a few more minutes and then sensed that Jake was ready to move to another area.

"C'mon," urged Jake, "check this out," and he led Jonathan and his small crew over to a tall shiny metal pole. The pole ran through a large hole in the ceiling down from the upper floor to the ground.

"Let me introduce you to Rolly. He's overseeing this event right now. You can see he's dressed in 'costume' so to speak to fit the spirit of our party tonight. Rolly," called Jake, "will you show the TV folks what's going on here."

Rolly turned to see where the voice was coming from and looked squarely into the TV camera. He was a big man whose outfit made him loom even larger and appear very imposing. He was dressed in full firefighting turnout gear which could be very scary if someone, especially a child, saw him walking through a fire toward them.

"Glad to," announced Rolly taking off his face shield and head gear. Then speaking into Jonathan's microphone, he explained, "we built this little scaffold here next to the pole so the kids can go up and slide down the same pole we use when we come down from the top floor. It's a shorter and less scary slide for the kids than sliding all the way through the hole in the ceiling.

"Then when they reach the bottom, they have to grab a uniform and get dressed into it as fast as they can."

"That uniform?" asked Jonathan pointing to a nearby pile of clothing on the floor, "It looks just like the one you're wearing. Do the kids have to dress up in that?" There were three neat piles of clothes lined up at the base of the pole. Each pile had a fire helmet on top of a full-length pair of coveralls (complete with red suspenders) which sat atop a pair of black rubber boots.

"Yeah, we had several sets made in different small sizes that will fit the kids. And they're just the basics. They don't include all this stuff," he said pointing to some of his gear. "The kids seem to love it and it's a riot watching them try to get into the outfits. But they really like sliding down the pole. Look at the line backing up."

Jonathan stood for a long while and watched as his sidekick filmed several children working their ways through the exercise. The laughter was non-stop. He finally turned and said "Yeah, thanks Rolly. What's next Jake?"

"Over there," answered Jake pointing to a far corner. "Sheila," he called to the monitoring firefighter, "Can you show Jonathan here what's going on. It's for TV."

"Of course," answered Sheila. "We're, ah, that is the kids are, putting out fires. We've attached water pistols to the ends of hoses that run over to the spigots in the kitchen sink. The kids take turns squirting water on those big lit candles there. It's like a little contest to see who can put their candle out the quickest."

Jonathan moved to the front of the line of kids and, again, stuck his microphone under the chin of a few. "So, is this fun?" he asked.

"Yeah!" was the loud chorus of young voices.

"I put my candle out first."

"I got mine out before you did."

"Yeah, but you squirted the wrong one so that didn't count."

Jonathan decided not to get into the middle of that discussion. He pulled his mic back and let the kids move up in line.

"This is all just an open house type of thing," explained Jake as they walked the floor. "People can come on their own time and can leave anytime they are ready to go. When they get ready to leave, each of the kids gets a goody bag filled with lots of cookies and stuff and a simple little gift. We all chipped in to fund this whole thing," he said.

"What a great gesture," replied Jonathan.

"Yeah, it is great. I think we have more fun watching and get more out of it than the kids do. I hope we can make it an annual thing. I'll let you folks walk around on your own, Jonathan. I'll go spell one of the other firefighters. Yell at me if you need anything."

Jonathan made a few more rounds of the floor, spoke to a lot of the families. The crew recorded a few kids' who gave answers to Jonathan's questions and filmed everything fully.

Over the course of the event, Jonathan noticed that he was enjoying himself. He became immersed a little bit in the whole idea and was impressed with what was going on. But he finally gave the word to turn off the equipment and get ready to take it out to load into the van.

"Uh, can I take a goody bag with me?" he asked before leaving the building. "You know, to use as a visual aid kind of thing back at the studio." The firefighter handing out the bags shook his head and grinned a little at Jonathan's feeble attempt to justify deserving a bag of goodies.

"Sure. Here you go. And he handed the reporter several bags. "Enough for your whole crew," he said, "and a few to, uh, to take back to the studio."

Once the TV crew was packed up and ready to hit the road, Jonathan stopped for a moment. He decided he wanted to go back inside and stay a little longer. He had driven directly from his house to the fire station in his own car, so he sent the rest of the crew back to the TV studio in the van. Then he headed back toward the door of the firehouse. But he was stopped there by a well-meaning firefighter who had just come on duty and was now passing out goody bags to exiting children.

"Captain Larson," the firefighter yelled after a few minutes' discussion with Jonathan. "Captain Larson, we have an issue here. Can you come help, please?"

'What is it?" asked the Chief as he hurried toward the door.

"This man wants to come into the party."

"So?"

"But he doesn't have a child with him as the price of admission."

Captain Larson led the burst of laughter that erupted from everyone who was within earshot.

༄

"OK, Margaret, back at'cha. Now it's your turn."

"Let's see," said Margaret as she continued to chuckle a little bit. "I would like to imagine a nice, homey, family Christmas." She looked over the village and finally focused on an inviting home that already had some outdoor decorations up. "That one," she said pointing. "Look there. I see a car that has pulled up in front and two elderly people are getting out of it."

XI

Grampa and Gramma have arrived at the house to begin their Christmas visit.

☙

It was only a second or two after they climbed out of the car that they were surrounded by some excited little people.

"Gramma! Grampa!" Screamed three children as they came running out of the house to greet their grandparents.

"Oh, my, my," exclaimed Gramma beaming with joy. "Look at the size of you kids. I swear you must have grown a foot since we saw you last." And she wrapped her arms as fully around all of them at once as much as the length of her arms would allow. "Do you recognize these big kids, Grampa?' she joked.

"Gramma, we just saw you last summer," reminded nine-year-old Denise. "We haven't grown that much since then," she corrected in all seriousness.

"I know honey. I'm teasing a little. I'm just really glad to see you. But what are you doing out here without your coats? C'mon let's get you back into the house where it's warm." And Gramma hurried them toward the door.

"Mom. It's Gramma and Grampa," shouted the kids as they burst through the door.

"I know, I know," Mom said as she held the door open and gave each one of her parents a hug as they came through it. "Let's let them come in and get settled down before you start to pester them," she instructed the kids.

A little later after luggage and packages had been carried in from the car and everyone had caught their breaths, the tether was loosened a bit and the kids unleashed their excitement. "What did you bring us Gramma?" asked Lydia and Daniel the six-year-old twins as they draped themselves over Gramma's lap.

"Bring you?" teased Gramma. "Why, it's Christmas time. It's not time to open gifts yet. You'll just have to wait until Christmas morning."

"Aww, Gramma," whined the kids. They were not really disappointed having expected some kind of answer like that.

"Did you see our decorations outside?" they asked next. "Daddy put them up on top of the roof last weekend. Aren't they pretty? They light up, too, and play music." Then, without waiting for a comment, they climbed out of Gramma's lap and kind of danced around the room aimlessly as if they could not sit still any longer. But they continued right on with their nonstop chatter.

"Did you bring us Christmas cookies?"

"Can we have one now?"

"We've been waiting for you to get here. Mommy said we had to wait for you before we could do things."

"Do things?" asked Gramma, "What kinds of things?"

"Well, Mommy said you would take us to see Santa," said Lydia.

"Oh, she did?"

"Yeah, and go shopping with us to get presents," added Denise.

"And put up some more decorations."

"And help us wrap presents."

"And drive around at night to see all the decorations."

"And go out for lunch."

"And play games."

"And watch movies."

"And make popcorn."

Grampa sat back and laughed at the energy and all the plans, but he didn't jump in to try and help Gramma respond to them all. Gramma looked over at him and gave him a pleading glance and a wry smile.

"I'll tell you what," said Gramma finally, "it's almost supper time. So, let's wait until after supper to think about all those things. We can figure them out later. In the meantime, are you old enough to set the table for supper? I'll bet your mom would like the help."

"I know how," bragged Denise.

"Good, then you can show the other two. Come and ask me if you need help but go wash your hands first." And off ran the children to get started on their new chore.

"Pretty clever," complimented Grampa. And he chuckled some more. Gramma got up and headed for the kitchen to explain why she had just made her daughter's meal preparation a little more difficult and the kitchen a little more crowded.

"Gramma, which side do the knives go on?" asked Denise.

"Does everyone get the little forks along with the big ones?" Lydia wanted to know.

"Are we supposed to use the fancy glasses tonight?" asked Daniel.

And so continued the chore until, "OK Mom, the table is all set."

"Thank you," praised their mother, "but supper isn't quite ready yet. Why don't you take Gramma and Grampa in and show them the tree?"

"Yeah, c'mon," squealed the twins. And off they dashed to the living room, but Gramma didn't follow.

"I'll be there in a minute," she called from a back room. "I do have something I can give you now and I want to get it."

A few minutes later she appeared in the doorway carrying a small package. She walked over to the couch, sat down, looked over at the lit tree and exclaimed, "My, what a pretty tree. Did you kids decorate it?"

"Well, Mom and Dad helped," explained Denise. "What's in the package, Gramma?"

"I brought along something special that you can keep and hang on your tree every year," and she began unwrapping the parcel on her lap. Having overheard the conversation, Mom came in from the kitchen to see what Gramma had. She leaned against the door frame with her arms folded and stayed in the background. Just at that point Dad came up from the basement and snuggled up beside her as they watched the kids crowd around Gramma.

"These are decorations that we used to hang on our tree when your mom was small. They were some of her favorites. They were each special because she made them herself." Gramma pulled out a very fancy, decorated foam ball, a pretty cloth and pipe cleaner angel and a three-dimensional star made out of colored beads.

"Oh, they're beautiful Gramma," exclaimed Denise. "I want the angel." And then the other two chimed in with, "I want the ball." "No, I want it." "You get the star." "No, you do."

"Woah," said Dad, "there's one for each of you and you can share. Now can you find room on the tree to hang each one up?

"Mom," said her daughter with a little tear in her eye, "that's so thoughtful of you. I didn't know you still had these." Then after a pause long enough for the kids to hang the ornaments, reposition each one two or three times and stand back to admire them, she announced that dinner was ready and to come to the table.

The excitement continued through the meal. The kids could hardly contain their exhilaration enough to eat. It finally came time for dessert and the kids asked to have one of the cookies that Gramma brought.

Gramma got up and fixed a plate of the cookies she wanted to let the kids try. They were brought out to the table along with coffee for the adults and a glass of milk for each of the kids.

"Ooh, Gramma, these cookies are too hard," complained Denise.

"Yeah, I can't even bite a piece off," added Lydia.

"How are you supposed to eat them?" asked Daniel.

"These cookies are made for dunking," explained Gramma. "They are supposed to be hard. So, you eat them by dunking them into your coffee for a few seconds before you take a bite—like this," and Gramma demonstrated how to do it. "Or into your milk. Try it but be careful not to drip or spill anything on the tablecloth."

"Ooh, weird," said Denise as she tried it, "but it works."

"I like them that way," said Lydia.

"Can I have another one?" asked Daniel. Everyone laughed and helped themselves to a second one also.

Dinner wrapped up, the dishes were washed, the kids got into their pajamas, and everyone gathered in the living room to visit around the tree a little more and to start the "calm down" process before it was time for the kids to go to bed. But the kids had other ideas. They were not going to calm down just because it was time. Questions flew and this time mostly at Grampa.

"What was your elf's name when you were a kid, Grampa?"

"My elf?"

"Yeah, your elf on the shelf. Ours is named Browney. He's over there on top of the bookcase watching us. We can't touch him, or he will disappear, and we won't get any presents."

"I see,' said Grampa. "I didn't have an elf when I was your age. There weren't any such things. Back then, at Christmas time, all the elves stayed hidden and wouldn't let anyone see them while they watched little children to see if they were being naughty or nice."

"What presents did you get back then?" Daniel wanted to know.

"Oh, I got things like a baseball glove or a sled or roller skates or a chemistry set. And I got a lot of clothes like socks and sweaters and shirts that I could wear to school."

"I want Legos this year," informed Daniel. "Did you get Legos?"

"No, there were no such things as Legos either. Instead, we had tinker toys or Lincoln Logs or erector sets."

"Did you and Gramma talk to each other on your cell phones when you were in school, Grampa?" Denise wanted to know.

"I didn't know Gramma yet when I was in school. But, no I didn't talk to anyone on a cell phone."

"Weren't you allowed to?"

"I didn't have a cell phone. No one had a cell phone then. They hadn't been invented yet."

"Then how did you call people?"

"We had a telephone in our house, but it was very much different than your cell phones are today. There was only one, and everyone had to take turns and share it if they wanted to call someone. And it couldn't move around because it was attached to the wall with a wire."

"They're not called telephones, Grampa, they're just phones," corrected Lydia.

"I see. Oh. And you know what? We didn't have a computer either."

The kids thought that over for a minute but then moved right on with their interrogation. "What's your favorite game to play, Grampa?"

"Oh, I don't know. I guess I like Checkers."

"No, I mean on the tablet."

"The tablet?" asked Grampa feigning ignorance.

"Yeah, what game did you like to play on your tablet when you were a kid?"

"I didn't have a tablet when I was a kid."

"Why? Wouldn't your daddy buy you one?"

"There were no such things as tablets back then either. Tablets were what they called some kinds of pills."

"Did you watch Frosty the Snowman or Rudolf on TV?"

"No. When I was your age, we didn't have a TV. They were brand new and cost a lot of money and only had three channels. We didn't get a TV until I was almost in High School. And you know what?"

"What?"

"All the shows were in black and white. They didn't have color TV yet."

"Oooh! No cell phone, no TV and no tablets. That would be boring. What did you do all day, Grampa?"

"Well, we played outside, rode our bikes, went swimming or ice skating and stuff like that. And we listened to the radio when our parents let us. Usually after dinner before bed."

"And with that," broke in Dad, "It's time for three young ones to be in bed. Tell your grandparents goodnight and let's head upstairs."

"Aww, Dad!"

"C'mon. Tomorrow is another day, and you'll have plenty of time to spend with them then."

On the way out of the living room Daniel was overheard to say to his twin sister, "I don't think Grampa had any fun way back when he was a kid. He didn't have any good things to play with like we have. He probably had to watch out for dinosaurs, too, so he wouldn't get stepped on."

ಸ

"Yes, I remember Christmases like that," smiled Shanice. "I wish they could all be like that. But, sadly," she continued after a moment, "not all of them are."

"No, not all of them are." Margaret then sat quietly for a minute and appeared to Shanice to be thinking seriously about something. "Speaking of nice homey family Christmas celebrations and kids," she finally said, "I have one more that came to mind while I was telling that last one. And I can't stop thinking about it. May I have an extra turn and imagine two in a row?"

"Go for it," encouraged Shanice.

XII

"I can imagine a family reunion that turns out... well, look into those windows over there and listen to the excited conversation.

❧

A just-past-middle-aged couple were sitting at the kitchen table finishing their supper.

"It's almost Christmas, Joe," announced Veronica.

"I know Vee," answered her husband.

"And I'm just so excited this year. I can hardly wait."

"How come?" asked Joe. "Christmases have become rather, oh, so, uh, 'routine' let's say. Just check off another one year after year lately."

"I know, I know, but this one is going to be special. I'm really looking forward to a real old fashioned family Christmas. You know like we used to have some years ago."

"I know what you mean but what's going to make this one like that?"

"The kids will all be home this year, for a change."

"How do you know that?"

"They've all told me so."

"When did they tell you so?" Joe wanted to know. "I haven't heard the phone ring recently. I didn't know you'd been in touch with any of them."

"Well, I haven't," admitted Veronica. "But each one of them has mentioned something about it over this past year."

"Over the past year? A lot of things can change over a year's time. What exactly did they say?"

"Oh, I can't remember exactly but Todd told me he would likely be able to get a pass from his sergeant this year. And Janene said she was looking forward to getting away from campus for a few days during her Christmas break this year."

"And, of course, Missy, our high school senior, will be here," added Joe with a chuckle. "After all she lives here. OK then, I guess we better plan on having a full house and a good old fashioned family Christmas. We really haven't all been together for the past couple of years—what with all the kids starting to go their separate ways."

"Yes," agreed Veronica. "They've become more and more independent as they've gotten older—just like we've taught them to be. But it'll be so good to spend some good old fashioned quality time with each of them. Kind of like getting to know each other again—not that we haven't stayed in touch with them."

"Yeah, but texts and emails don't exactly let you stay very close to one another. Even phone calls aren't like dinner table conversations," agreed Joe. "But you're right. It will be good to all be together again and to catch up with each other."

"Joe, let's decorate everything just like we used to. You know, the tree and wreaths and candles and garlands and bows and outside lights and, well, you know. Everything."

"Gussied up to the hilt, eh," joked Joe.

"I know!" added Veronica gleefully. "Remember when we used to do that snowman display outside? Is that still around somewhere?"

"Yeah, it's put away in the attic."

"Then let's put it up this year. The house will look just like it did when the kids were small. I bet they'll really be surprised when they see it."

"Well, I guess I've got a lot of work to do then. I better get started on it—uh, first thing tomorrow."

"And I'm going to plan some special meals and activities. I'm even going to do some baking just like I used to," said Veronica excitedly. "Cookies and cakes and pies. Ooh, Joe, I can hardly wait."

"I know. You said that already." And he quickly added before his wife could feel insulted by his remark,

"I can hardly wait either. I really am starting to get excited, too."

As the day drew closer for the family to start to gather the excitement heightened.

"Todd is coming home today," reminded Veronica. "He's taking the bus. I'll call later to check the expected arrival time."

"That would be a good idea," advised Joe. "I just heard on the news that there's a big snowstorm heading across the state up north. On the map it looks like it will cut right across the bus route between here and Fort Hart. There may be some delays. Fortunately, it's not supposed to drift very far down our way. Once he's through the snow it should be smooth sailing the rest of the way here."

Later that day Veronica dejectedly updated Joe on Todd's progress. "The storm has apparently blown up into something pretty big," she explained. "I can reach no one at the bus station and they don't answer their phones at the company headquarters. I did reach Todd on his cell phone. He's on the bus somewhere right about in the middle of the storm and we didn't have a very clear connection. It sounded like they are still moving but they're down to a crawl. The roads are deep in snow and the holiday traffic is mostly off in the ditches. He has no idea of what time they may get in but if they don't get stuck in a drift or slide off the road, he thinks it will probably be late tonight. He said not to wait up for him. He'll take a cab home and see us in the morning."

"OK, we'll leave the door unlocked and a light on for him. His room is ready, so he'll probably walk in and head straight to bed. Don't worry about him, Vee. I'm sure he'll be OK. He's a smart young man. He knows how to take care of himself."

When Todd finally got himself out of bed late the next morning he showered, shaved, dressed and headed to the kitchen for breakfast. After the hugs and the usual reunification ritual he sat down to a big breakfast that his mother had gone out of her way to prepare. In the course of conversation, as he ate, he casually said, "I hope it's OK if I take the car today."

"The car?" asked Joe. "Uh, sure, if you have to run some errands. How long will you need it?"

"Not sure. Probably all day. I don't expect to get back until late tonight."

"What?" exclaimed his mother in an obviously disappointed tone of voice.

"I'm sorry, Mom."

"But Todd, you just got home. I thought you and your father would watch the ball game together. And I'm ready to fix your favorite dinner tonight. I hoped we could all sit and talk a while and maybe play a board game or two—you know like we used to."

"Yeah, that would be fun, Mom, but remember Caleb? Well, he got hurt pretty bad in a training accident and can't get out of the hospital to get home this year. I promised him I would look up his parents and try to reassure them that he'll be alright soon. There is no way they can get up to the post hospital."

"Oh, yeah. Of course, you have to do that. I understand."

"And then, I promised Ronny I'd come visit when I got home. I haven't seen him since high school. And he got us tickets to the hockey game tonight."

Veronica issued a soft but slightly audible groan. "Well, I suppose I can postpone the dinner until tomorrow night," she sighed.

"Uh, Mom, I'm afraid I've got a little more bad news. During that ride home yesterday, I got a text from my sergeant announcing that all leaves were canceled. Everyone has been called back to base for an emergency security situation that seems to be developing. I don't know what it is. It's too late to get the bus back today but I have to catch it tomorrow morning. I'm sorry but I won't be able to stay."

"Oh, Todd, I'm sorry," said his mother. She paused for a moment, then added, "but I understand. We'll try to all get together again another time." She tried hard not to show her disappointment though Todd could have recognized it in her voice. But he didn't.

"Well, it's not coming together like I had planned," Veronica said to Joe after Todd had left the house.

"I know," said Joe sympathetically, "but at least most of the family will be together for Christmas. Janene and Missy will be here with us."

At that point the land line phone rang. Joe answered it. "Hi Janene," he gushed into it. "You sound pretty bubbly. OK, yeah, here, I'll let you talk to your mother."

Veronica took the phone and offered a cheery 'Hello' into it. Then after a few seconds of listening intently to her daughter on the other end her expression dropped and she replied, "What? Oh, no Janene. I was so counting on you being home this year. I thought you and Missy and I could go to town to watch the Christmas Pageant at the Music Hall this year. Yes... yes... yes, I understand. I'm sure you are excited. Yes, you should be. Well, you have a good time and do a good job. We'll be anxious to hear all about it when you get back. Yes, love you, too. Goodbye." And she switched off the phone and handed it back to Joe who was anxiously awaiting an explanation.

"She won't be coming home this year," explained Veronica. "The concert that her choir is performing in London has been moved up and she has to be on the plane with the whole group tomorrow."

"But..." started Joe. "We've known about that choir tour for a long time now. It isn't scheduled until after Christmas."

"She said something in London apparently changed with the theater availability. Something about another group having to cancel at the last minute. They want Janene's university choir to fill in for them which moved the date up. But that means now they will stay on for an extra week and add several more performances. The London company is going to compensate them for all the extra expense of coming early."

"Hm. I guess it will be a great experience for her," suggested Joe consolingly, "and it will certainly be a boon for the choir and the school."

"Yeah," sighed Veronica. She took a deep breath and as she turned to leave the room she uttered, "but it will be a bust for our family Christmas."

So the excitement diminished a little but everything had been gotten ready so there was nothing left to rush around about. It was only two days before Christmas Eve.

Just as Veronica was starting to put dinner on the table that evening, Missy came running in. She had been gone the whole day helping a neighbor down the street. "Mom, Mom, guess what," she screamed excitedly as she ran up to her mother. "I'm going to Disney World for Christmas."

"You're what?" asked Veronica in a surprised raised voice.

"I'm going to Disney World for Christmas!"

"I know what you said. I heard you but just what do you mean by that statement?"

"Well, the Jacobsens whole family has reservations for Disney World over Christmas. They leave tomorrow on the day before Christmas Eve."

"Yes, and?"

"And they were going to take Cynthia along to look after the children. You know at times when the adults want to go out alone."

"Cynthia? Your classmate Cynthia?"

"Yes. Anyway, Cynthia has come down sick just today and told them she would not be able to go along. And guess what. Mrs. Jacobsen asked me if I would like to go and be their babysitter. I told them yes! Isn't that great?"

"Yes, Missy, that is great. But don't you think you should have checked with us first?"

"Oh, yeah, maybe. But Mom I'm a senior in high school. I'm almost in college and I should be able to make my own decisions."

"Well, we'll talk about that some other time, young lady. But I do know the Jacobsens very well and it is a very good opportunity for you that might not otherwise come along again for quite some time. So, you may go." But, once again, Veronica's voice betrayed a sad disappointment.

Then at the end of the next day, after seeing Missy off to Disney World, the two parents found themselves alone again.

"Well, here we are Joe. Just you and me again," said Veronica sarcastically as the two of them stood and gazed out the window. The night was dark but their yard decorations were aglow.

"Don't you mean the three of us?" Joe asked

"What do you mean the three of us? It's just you and me," corrected Veronica sternly.

"You and me and the snowman there," said Joe pointing out the window at the big smiling yard decoration with its white lights twinkling on and off just like in former days when the kids' faces would light up staring at it. Joe was trying to lighten the mood a little. Instead, his little joke caused Veronica to miss the kids just that much more. She turned into Joe's arms and cuddled there trying hard not to cry.

"I miss them too, Vee," said Joe, "but it'll all be OK. We've given them roots. Now they're starting to try out their new wings. Everything's just like it's supposed to be. I think we've done a good job as parents."

"Yeah, I guess we have, haven't we," agreed Veronica. "It just seems like it all flew by so fast. I suppose I'll get used to it all eventually." She paused for a long minute. "But right now, Joe, I'm still sad.

"And lonesome for the family Christmas that almost was."

ಈ

"I'm sorry," apologized Margaret after her story was finished for adding such a somber note to the evening."

"Not at all," argued Shanice. "Your story is real life, and it definitely has a place during the season. *But* now it's my turn to apologize in advance because there is another darker Christmas story that I hear a lot about these days. It keeps coming back to haunt me a little and I think it, too, needs to be told while we're looking inside the little village. It is my turn so please bear with me. There," she said pointing to one of the houses. "There in the back is an apartment a little like the one over the craft store except a little more upscale."

XIII

Shanice paused for a minute before beginning her story. She was trying to figure out how to tell a dark story without turning the holiday completely ugly for Margaret. Finally, she began.

༄

"Why can't Dad come home for Christmas?" pleaded Angel.

"He just can't," snapped her mother.

"But, Mom, I want him to come home," whined the teen.

"I'm sorry, Angel, he cannot. He won't. This isn't his home anymore."

"But, Mom, it's Christmas."

"Now look, we've been over this before, and I don't have time for it again," scolded her mother in an impatient and ugly voice. "Rick will be here any minute now and I have to be ready to go,"

"Rick? Is that your latest boyfriend? How long will this one last?" screamed Angel and she ran off to her bedroom slamming the door behind her.

"Oh, that kid," growled her mother absently but out loud. "It's about time she got over this. But I can't worry about it now."

"You never seem to have time to worry about it," interrupted Susan as she walked into the room. She had overheard the whole conversation from another room. "Angel is your daughter and my younger sister, and she needs us both right now. She's having a hard time."

"Don't you get sassy with me, young lady," berated her mother. "Oh, there's the door. Rick is here and I have to go. Both of you just deal with it." And she put on a big smile and a fluttery voice as she opened the door and stepped out of the apartment to meet her date.

Susan walked over to the bedroom door, knocked on it and asked, "Angel, may I come in?"

"No! Go away!"

"It's just me, Angel. Mom's gone."

"I don't want to talk to anyone," screamed Angel. "Just go away. I want to be alone."

But Susan was concerned about her sister and a little agitated herself. "Angel this is my room, too. We share it, remember? I'm coming in." And Susan pushed hard against the door that tended to stick when it was closed.

When Susan entered the room Angel jumped up, rushed at her sister and pushed her back onto the bed. In the process Angel screamed, "I can't take it anymore. I have to get out of this house." And Angel jammed the door shut behind her as she ran out of the bedroom and headed to the front door."

"Angel!" yelled Susan while trying to untangle herself from the bed. "Stop! What are you doing? Where are you going?"

"I don't know," screamed Angel. "Just out. Anywhere. I have to get away." And with that she continued to stomp across the room, her eyes streaming with tears. She jerked open the apartment door and tore out slamming it as she left.

Susan became very scared at Angel's reply. She had never threatened anything like that before—especially leaving. She did her best to follow but her sister had a head start and was on a tear. Susan ran outside and into the street. Not paying attention to anything except trying to spot Angel, she ran smack into a man and a woman walking along the sidewalk.

"Oh, excuse me," she apologized in somewhat of a panic, "I'm sorry. But I'm looking for my sister and it's very important. Did you happen to see a girl run through here just a few seconds ago?"

"As a matter of fact, a young girl did rush past us," answered the woman. "She ran around to the back of the building and disappeared in the dark."

"Thank you," said Susan hurriedly, "I must find her." And Susan turned ready to dash off.

"May we help?" asked the man before Susan could get away.

"I, uh, no, uh I uh…"

"You go. We'll follow you. Maybe, together, we can find her more quickly."

Susan hurried off.

After a short search the man called to Susan. "I think we may have found your sister. Is this her?" and he called Susan over to the open door of a garage behind the girls' apartment building. "We heard crying coming from inside." The couple followed Susan into the garage as she headed toward the sound of crying coming from a dark corner along the back wall.

The three came upon the girl hiding in the dark, sitting on the floor with her head between knees that were pulled up in front of her. "My word," gasped the woman with a little surprise, "Is everything OK? No, of course it isn't. I'm sorry. What can we do to help?"

Susan paused a minute and took a little step back. She didn't know how to respond to the question. Who were these strange people and what right did they have getting involved in other people's business? Did she dare trust them? But she quickly decided there was no other good alternative at the moment, and she could use help. She couldn't handle this alone. She had to trust what she hoped were good Samaritans.

"Thank you," offered Susan. "This is Angel, and she is having a hard time this Christmas."

Before Susan could explain more, the woman took her by the elbow and gently nudged her up to the front of the garage and out of Angel's hearing. As she did so she quietly motioned to the man to stay close to Angel so she could not run away. Once near the open door of the garage the woman explained to Susan, "I'm not sure what you're going to tell me, but I got the feeling it might be personal, and I thought it might not be right to talk about it in front of your sister."

"I want my daddy," wailed Angel loudly sobbing from inside her dark safe zone in the garage, and she returned her head back to between her knees.

"Where is her father?" asked the woman. "Can we go get him?"

"No. That's not possible. We don't know where he is. He just left us some time ago. Angel has taken it pretty hard."

"What about your mother?" asked the woman. "Oh, I'm sorry," she added, "I know this isn't any of our business. I shouldn't ask."

"It's alright," answered Susan in a quiet voice, happy to have someone to talk to for a change and she just let her guard down a bit and let everything come out. "Since Dad left, Mom has kind of rebelled, I guess, by trying to find the life she used to have before we both came along."

"Oh!" exclaimed the woman. "I see. And Angel feels the stress of all that very deeply."

"Yes, ma'am," answered Susan. Her trust in the couple was growing. "But there's more," she confided. She had kept it all bottled up inside too long.

"More?"

"Yes, on top of all that, Angel is kind of a target for some of the girls at school. She gets teased a lot—about her name, for example, and her weight even though she is not too heavy."

"She has a very beautiful name. How can they tease her about that?"

"She gets called a 'chubby cherub' or they say, when she can hear them, 'I never heard of a fat Angel' and they post on the internet that she would be better off going back to heaven where angels belong."

"That's so sad. And so unnecessary. I'm sorry."

Susan continued, "They had a special student activity day at the school the other day. I found the painting she did thrown in the trash can. I thought it was very good, but someone told her she paints like a first grader. Then her boyfriend ignored her, and she watched him take another girl to the basketball game. She just left in tears without going to the craft sale or the concert."

"I can see the problem here," said the woman. "May I get involved a little? I may be able to help some, though I'm no expert."

"If you can, yes, please do. I would appreciate it very much. By the way, my name is Susan. I'm a couple of years older than Angel. Maybe that's why I haven't been upset as much about things. But I'm worried for my sister. Her self-esteem has just dropped to a very low spot. I think maybe Christmas makes it all a little worse, too, because it's a happy season for everyone else but not for Angel."

"Yes, I recognize that. Sadness and depression can be very real for some people this time of the year. To start with, I think she needs a friend. Maybe I can be that." She looked back into the garage at the man and reassured herself that he would support what his wife was about to suggest. She and Susan walked back into the dark space where Angel still sat.

"Angel?" she called softly after stooping down close to the girl. No answer.

"Angel?"

"What?"

"Angel, my name is Robin. You don't know me because we have just moved to town. I am a new teacher at your school. I will start after the holiday break at the beginning of the next term. This is my husband, Martin. We would like to be your friends."

"I don't have any friends."

"That's why we would like to be the first. You are very important, and we would like to get to know you. Can we do that?"

There was a long silence during which Angel seemed to be thinking deeply. There seemed to be something about these people—maybe their demeanor or the tone of their voices or their concern—that she could not argue with as hard as she tried. Finally, a small soft voice answered, "yes."

"Great," replied Robin gently. "Can you stand up so we can see you. I'd like to give you a hug."

As Susan stood back and watched, Angel sniffed, wiped her eyes, brushed back the hair from her face and stood up to face Robin. Robin reached out both arms to her and Angel slowly stepped into them. Robin pulled her close into a comfortable hug.

"Girls," said Robin a minute or so later—after Angel had backed a step away, "I would like to show you where we live because I would like you to come visit me every day between now and when school starts back up. Is your mother available tonight?"

"No, she is out on a date somewhere. We don't know where," explained Susan.

"Then how about walking with us right now so you will know where to come tomorrow?" And the four started to walk away together.

As they walked Angel found the unexpected courage to ask, "May I hold your hand?"

"Of course," answered Robin. "Tell you what, why don't all of us hold hands?"

And as they stepped into the street because the sidewalk was too narrow, the four of them walked side by side and hand in hand the short distance to the apartment above Mrs. Mapleton's craft shop.

∽

As Shanice's story ended Margaret just sat in still silence for a few minutes. She was obviously thinking about what she had just heard and about a side of Christmas that very few ever know about or can imagine. Finally, Margaret said, "You're right Shanice, that is a dark side of this holiday. Depression is real and Christmas doesn't make it go away. But I guess it gets pushed into the background because it's a hard thing to think about.

"Maybe that's where we should leave our story telling for tonight. What do you think? Should we end it on that note?"

"Not quite yet," came a voice from the back corner of the room. "I think there's one more story that needs to be told before the evening ends."

The football game had ended, and the husbands had come looking for the ladies. When they saw what was going on they quietly entered the room and stood in the back listening until Shanice had finished her story. The ladies had not noticed them until Shanice's husband, Tobin, spoke up.

"And I'm going to be the one to tell it," he said as he walked over to the miniature village. Rudy followed, sat down next to Margaret and gave his wife a smile.

Tobin stooped down to search the buildings. "Ah, there," he said and pointed to the wooded area of the display. "Look into the bright windows of that old wooden church. It is Christmas Eve, after all.

"Look who's walking through the front door."

XIV

Four people have completed their short walk along the dark wooded path and are approaching the welcoming lights of an old wooden structure.

☙

"Welcome to our late-night Christmas Eve service," said a friendly voice. "Please come inside" and the man held the door open for the four newcomers. "I'm Werner Hochhimmel, the pastor this evening."

The pleasant, older man was dressed in business casual clothing—no robe, but he wore a white clergy collar. Near the door, but inside against the back wall, was a life sized creche with full sized shepherds and wise men squeezed in. It crowded the small vestibule and prevented it from being a good place for folks to gather and visit.

Not being familiar with local customs, Martin, Robin, Susan, and Angel had arrived early to be sure to get a seat. So, very few people had yet arrived, and those who had were all inside the sanctuary. It was not too inconvenient, then, for the four to linger near the door a moment to talk with the pastor.

With a questioning glance Martin asked, "You said 'Pastor for this evening'?"

"Oh, yes," smiled Werner, "I'm sorry. You must be new in town. Let me explain. You see this old church dates back to the very early days of our little community. It became outdated many years ago. But it has a fond place in the hearts of the townspeople who do not want it to fall into disrepair. It is not used anymore on a regular weekly basis or for food preparation events, but all the churches in town have joined together to preserve it as a nondenominational chapel for use on special occasions. We all schedule our combined Christmas Eve services and other special events to take place in this building. The ministers of the various churches rotate as the presiding pastor here on those occasions. This year I happen to have the privilege of serving tonight."

"What a great idea. It looks like a very comfortable and welcoming place," said Robin. "And I love this manger scene. It's beautiful."

"Yes, thank you. I wish we could set it outdoors so it could speak to more people but, I'm afraid, we must confine it to its spot right here."

"Why is that? Asked Martin.

"Well, sadly, there have come to be many people who see it as an insult and an imposition on their personal beliefs. Consequently, there are those who protest by damaging or stealing parts of the display. So, to protect it and to preserve it for those to whom it has such sacred meaning we have to move it indoors."

"That's such a shame," said Robin.

"Yes," said Martin, "it is sad. I guess it's for that same reason that churches today have to keep their doors locked all the time."

"Uh, yes. But this is not the time to be morose. Who are these young ladies?"

"This is Susan," said Robin indicating the older sister, "and this is Angel."

"Angel? What a beautiful and special name," replied pastor Hochhimmel. "And you are?"

"Oh, I'm sorry. My name is Robin, and this is my husband, Martin. We've just moved to town."

"It's nice to meet you all. Please come in and make yourselves comfortable. The service will begin shortly."

The rustic structure was sparsely but appropriately decorated for the season. There was an old upright piano up front near a split-log altar rail with a free-standing lectern behind it that served as a pulpit. Martin and the girls found seats on one of the long wooden planks that were the pews, and it wasn't long before they were closely bracketed by other worshippers.

They made use of the time to introduce themselves and become acquainted with new neighbors.

The little church soon filled with people and the density of the crowd increased the room's warmth whose heat, otherwise, came from the building's wood-burning stove. For safety reasons the original gas lamps had been replaced by electric lighting some years ago but the old-fashioned appearance of the new fixtures had been preserved.

Finally, the piano called the service to order. The celebration followed the pattern typical for Christmas Eve. There were carols, readings recalling the Biblical events, prayers and of course an appropriate, uplifting sermon.

"Amen" pronounced the pastor at the end of his message. "But before we sing our last hymn let me add a few more words of personal opinion.

"It occurred to me many years ago, while sitting in a driver's education class, that the words I was hearing were not exclusively, but were predominantly, used in that particular sector of life. Common words that were not used very much in other disciplines and were somewhat strange to me at that time. Words like yield, right-of-way, U-turn, center line, accelerate. I realized the same is true for other disciplines with words like cathode or current or resistance when speaking about electricity. Or caliber, rank-and-file, cadre, or camouflage in the military. Words that you don't hear much like deposit, withholding, escrow, or vested except when speaking of financial or banking matters.

"And the same is true for this season of the year. But, to me, some of the words and phrases of Christmas are the most poetic and beautiful of all the others, especially when used together to express an emotion. They are even more so when spoken in the vernacular of King James. When you hear them you just automatically think 'Christmas'. So, take a few moments to think about them after you leave here tonight, and while you celebrate the rest of this holiday. They are words and phrases like...

"Swaddling clothes..."

"Manger..."

"Gold. Frankincense. Myrrh..."

The pastor pronounced each slowly, deliberately and with appropriate inflection and emotion—pausing briefly between each.

"And it came to pass..."

"And she brought forth her firstborn..."

"Shepherds abiding in the field..."

"And, lo, the angel of the Lord came upon them, and the glory of the Lord shone round about them: and they were sore afraid..."

"Behold, I bring you good tidings of great joy..."

"For unto you is born this day in the city of David a Savior..."

"And suddenly there was with the angel a multitude of heavenly host..."

"Glory to God in the highest, and on earth peace, good will toward men…"

"And so many more," concluded the pastor. He paused for a few seconds to emphasize the peace that had been growing throughout this special evening.

Then he continued, "In the interest of safety and fire prevention in this wooden structure please gather outdoors where we will continue the tradition of lighting our individual candles while we sing Silent Night. Pick up a candle from the basket as you go out the door. Following the end of the hymn please extinguish your candle and proceed in silence away from the building as you make your way back to your homes on this sacred night."

And so, as the words of their hymn drifted off into the dark, chill air, the villagers faded into the night in anticipation of the arrival of Christmas morn.

☙

The end of Tobin's story marked the end of a nice evening for Shanice and Margaret and the couples headed for the front door to wish each other a fond goodnight and part company. But, as is the way with long good-byes, the conversations couldn't seem to find a stopping place and neither couple made the effort to be the first to turn the door knob. So, they lingered.

XV

Mrs. McLaughlin was an elderly woman who had outlived all of her family except one distant relative who was located clear across the country. She had no friends or visitors anymore, so was alone in the world. She now spent her days as a resident of Hilltop House, an elder care facility.

Of the seasonal decorations the staff had set out, her favorite was a little winter village scene displayed on a low coffee table in the middle of the common room. One of Mrs. McLaughlin's favorite things to do at this time of year, was to sit and gaze at the little buildings. She was happy spending most of her day in that way, day after day after day. It somehow took her back to her earlier years and she took much pleasure in remembering. Remembering, oh, so many pleasant things. Things that came back to life for her, though she couldn't remember, sometimes, if they were always real or maybe imaginary. That didn't matter to Mrs. McLaughlin.

On this particular night she was alone in the room. The room lights had been dimmed and the little winter scene on the coffee table cast faint shadows around its little pretend neighborhood by way of the glowing lights shining out through the building's windows. Mrs. McLaughlin sat close to the table and bent as low over it as she was able. For a little while she was in her own little world—a world of Christmases past and so many memories. She eventually and slowly returned from her reverie and sat up straight.

"Goodnight, ladies, and thank you again," she said as she backed away from the display and the bright windows of its small central ceramic house wherein her imaginary friends, Shanice and Margaret, were exchanging imaginary tales.

And the old woman turned her wheelchair around and headed for her room and bed with a happy, peaceful smile on her face.